ALL CREEPING THINGS

Britney Everlong

To Alex, Parker, and Lukas.

Britney Everlong

May 27, 2022

Prelude

"...And Noah did according unto all that the Lord had commanded him. And Noah was six hundred years old when the flood of waters was upon the earth. And Noah went in, and his sons, and his wife, and his sons' wives with him, into the ark, because of the waters of the flood. Of clean beasts, and of beasts that are not clean, and of fowls, and of every thing that creepeth upon the earth, there went in two and two unto Noah into the ark, as God had commanded Noah."

-Genesis 7:5-9

Silence filled the crater once the echoes of the impact had finished ringing. The fires had begun to rage in the distance even before the waters could collapse back down into their proper place. Still, before everything could crash back into the place it belonged, there was the preternatural silence. It was a stillness that this small world had never known, the kind of stillness that only precedes the ride of Death and his horsemen. Civilization was still new to this world, and the oncoming destruction was beyond their ability to understand.

In the blazing heart of the crater, molten rock from both earth and space intertwined in a dance of near-plasmic heat, blasting forth in a fountain that reached back into space. The fire at the very heart of the world belched forth into the ether, freezing solid upon contact with the lethal cold of space and plummeting back to the ground. The very firmament seemed to shake with its fury, and the mountains cracked, and some even crumbled in the wake of the horrible impact.

And then gravity, seemingly holding its breath in shock, remembered its duty, and brought the sea back down.

The tsunamis that swelled up from that point were unlike any the world had ever seen. They tore across land and sea equally, some reaching such terrifying heights that they could travel far enough inland to slaughter creatures that had no idea such a thing as a sea even existed. Walls of water, travelling at speeds unimaginable, standing miles high, scoured the land clean, and left the planet a flooded, barren rock, save for the few places where life clung to the highest of high ground.

Fire and water cleansed the small world, and it was good in her sight.

Chapter One

"Not everyone who says to me, 'Lord, Lord,' will enter the kingdom of heaven, but the one who does the will of my Father who is in heaven. On that day many will say to me, 'Lord, Lord, did we not prophesy in your name, and cast out demons in your name, and do many mighty works in your name?' And then will I declare to them, 'I never knew you; depart from me, you workers of lawlessness."

-Matthew 7:21-23

The first rays of dawn began to reflect off the morning dew, and already the smell of hot tea and toast wafted out of the kitchen of the modest house on a nondescript corner in a nondescript neighborhood. It was the custom for the house's sole occupant to rise early; his life was filled with long stretches of study, with the occasional glut of frenetic activity, so in either case it suited him to get an early start.

He sat at his kitchen table, sipping quietly from a cup of steaming herbal tea. A thick, old book sat open in front of him, one he eagerly poured through even as the fine crumbs of wheat toast fell to the yellowed pages, an indiscretion to which he seemed to remain oblivious. Old woodcut prints lined the pages of eldritch and arcane things that few who worked outside his field would even begin to understand. Thus was the life of the Biblical archaeologist; he had spent his life fighting against an ever more secular society to prove that the word of God was real, that the acts of Jesus and His apostles actually happened, and worked his tail off, only to still be looked upon as somewhat of a crackpot by more "mainstream" archaeologists, who apparently were more concerned with proving that the Egyptians were aliens, or some other such nonsense.

Still, it hadn't been without victories. He'd smiled on the day they'd found Jericho's walls. A small triumph for his field, but a great victory for the Lord had been won on that day. It was enough for Innocent Nsabimana then, and it was still enough for him as he enjoyed his morning tea.

However, sweet as the victories were, they were infrequent, and becoming harder each day to offset the growing pile of rejection letters for the grants he'd applied for that sat nearby. Biblical archaeology was, unfortunately, bordering on fringe in modern academia, and Innocent himself had garnered a reputation amongst archaeologists for being a bit of, for lack of a better term, a lunatic.

Innocent ascribed to the school of theological belief that the world was actually around six thousand years old, as calculated by the ages of the Old Testament patriarchs and taught by such luminaries as Ken Ham, Henry Morris, and others. Many of Innocent's colleagues considered it pseudoscience and even laughable, though they considered Innocent himself an intelligent man, and a fine archaeologist. His body of work was impressive, but many organizations that paid out grants just didn't want to be associated with a delusional fundamentalist. Innocent took the barbs and stones with grace; he knew the Lord would not forsake him. He just had to be patient and to have faith that He had a plan.

Thus it was on that morning; Innocent, as ever, sat at his table, musty old book open at his right hand, grant application at his left, tea and toast in the middle, and the first rays of morning making him feel as if the Lord Himself was smiling on him. The scent of hibiscus tea infused with cinnamon and Thai chilies wafted through the air, and the smell of the toast came shortly after. It was a good morning, even after being turned down for two more grants. His department desperately needed the money, but he trusted in the Lord. It would come, somehow.

From the living room, a muted bleeping sound signaled that a phone call was incoming. Innocent's heart lifted slightly, as a phone call at this time of the morning was rarely bad news. He gulped down a healthy sip of tea and rose to go into the living room, catching his foot on the leg of his chair, nearly tripping and falling on his face. He managed to catch himself before that could happen, and, laughing at his clumsiness, stumbled awkwardly into the living room.

"'Allo?" Innocent spoke, in his still-thick Rwandan accent. Though he'd been in the United States for several years, he still spoke very much like the Tutsi man he had always been, and he had little desire to stop being who he was.

"Doctor Nsabimana?" At twenty-seven years old, Innocent was the youngest professor at Wheaton College. He'd actually tested out of high school upon arriving in the States at sixteen and received his Ph.D. at twenty-three. He'd been hailed as quite the prodigy at Cornell, where he'd done his undergraduate work, and upon receiving his Ph.D. at Harvard, the world seemed quite literally at his feet, at least until his religious views started becoming public.

"Yes, this is he. To whom am I speaking?"

"Doctor Nsabimana, my name is Gerald Tyler, and I represent a consortium of individuals who, like yourself, are interested in Biblical discoveries," the man on the phone said, in a measured and proper English cadence. "They, also like yourself, have a large stake in proving that the true Word of God is accurate."

Innocent's interest was piqued. "I'm listening."

"There has recently been a discovery in a Solomonic-era tomb, just entered in the last few days," Tyler continued. "An ancient papyrus document discussing the jewel that fell from Lucifer's crown as he fell from Heaven."

Innocent's pulse quickened with anticipation. Surely there was no way…

"It also reveals the location of where the jewel fell, Doctor. And more; it reveals where Lucifer himself fell."

Innocent gasped as the blood rushed out of his face. "Surely not…"

Tyler continued, as calmly as before. "We cannot verify anything without excavating these sites, Doctor, and we cannot get permission to excavate without an accredited scholar attached to the expedition. You, Doctor Nsabimana, come most highly recommended. You will be quite well compensated for your time, and your name will be the one in the journals. It will, I do believe, erase all doubt about you over your religious oddity."

Innocent held the phone to his ear silently as he considered the offer. To regain his reputation as an archaeologist would be priceless, and to discover such a find as Lucifer's crown jewel would do far more than regain his lost reputation; it would be indisputable proof of Lucifer's fall, and by association, the Bible itself. However, the idea of going to a site as certainly unholy as the site of Lucifer's fall gave him pause, but many had walked boldly into worse for the sake of Christ. Could he do any less?

"I accept your offer, Mr. Tyler."

"A wise choice, Doctor Nsabimana. Please get what you need to arrange done so by tomorrow morning, ten o'clock Chicago time. A car will be sent for you."

Tyler ended the call, and Innocent beamed with joy at the notion of the adventure to come. He'd sensed that today would bring good news, and he of course knew that God works in mysterious ways, but he'd never expected such a thing to land so squarely in his lap. He took a satisfied sip of his tea and smiled broadly as the sun shone over Glen Allyn, bringing its light once more to his neighborhood.

Chapter Two

Innocent was scurrying about his house, getting things packed. Though he knew nothing about this alleged consortium that was hiring him, a cursory search of the Internet yielded quite a bit of information on Gerald Tyler. Tyler was a well-known artifact hunter, specializing in Biblical archaeological finds. He had been present on the dig that discovered the walls of Jericho, and had been part of digs at Hazor, Megiddo, and Tanis. He was well-respected in the archaeological community, which of course led Innocent to the inevitable question; why did Tyler need *him*?

There wasn't time for such thinking, though, as the appointed hour grew close. Innocent threw the last few bits of clothing he could think of needing into his duffel and zipped it closed with alacrity; excitement was overcoming him. The crown of Lucifer was, of course, considered to be apocryphal, and not well-known, even among Christians, but the notion that the jewel that fell from it could exist filled Innocent with equal parts zeal and terror. If the jewel was real, then the crown was real, and if the crown was real…

Then Lucifer himself was real, and the Apocalypse was truly coming.

After six thousand years, the final judgment of humanity would be nigh, and would it be known that he, Doctor Innocent Nsabimana, Ph.D., had played a hand in showing the glory of the Most High?

Innocent shook off such thinking quickly, dismissing it as pure vanity. It was a dangerous path he tread now, that path between doing something for the glory of God and for his own glory. He calmed himself, remembering why he was doing what he was doing, and grabbed his duffel, walking to the front room of his home, waiting for the car that was supposed to collect him.

Without fail, at the stroke of ten o'clock, a sleek car, black in color with tinted windows, pulled up in front of Innocent's home. It was not a limousine, but it was still an expensive-looking vehicle. It waited for him to exit the house. Innocent did not make them wait long; he practically came leaping forth from his home as soon as the car arrived. Once Innocent exited the house, a man in a dark suit exited the front passenger side door, and took Innocent's duffel, loading it into the trunk of the car, and opened the back passenger door for him. Innocent quickly entered to see Gerald Tyler himself sitting on the opposite side, a broad smile on his face, a far more kindly expression than his tone during their conversation had implied. The man who had opened the door for Innocent closed the door, and then got in himself, and closed his door. Once he had done so, the car drove off, and Gerald Tyler extended his hand in greeting.

"Doctor Nsabimana, it's good to finally meet you," Tyler said. "You come very highly recommended."

"And you, Mr. Tyler," Innocent replied. "Your name is quite well known amongst Biblical scholars."

Tyler chuckled mirthfully. "I am no scholar, Doctor Nsabimana. I am merely a man who wishes to know truth."

"Is that not what a scholar is, Mr. Tyler?"

Tyler chuckled again. "Perhaps. Perhaps. So, to business, yes?"

Innocent nodded. "Please."

Tyler pulled a folded sheet of paper from the inside pocket of his suit jacket. He unfolded it to reveal a stunning copy, in full color, of what appeared to be an ancient sheet of papyrus with strange diagrams on it, and odd writing around the diagrams. He handed the copy to Innocent, who looked it over with astonishment.

"I have never seen anything like this, Mr. Tyler."

"If I am to be honest, Doctor, no one has," Tyler replied. "You can see it is inscribed in Sumerian, which is generally not written on papyrus, as they did not have such technology to our knowledge, so someone in Solomonic times knew a dead language and chose to use it to inscribe this."

Innocent read the cuneiform script, his lips moving silently to the translation running through his mind. The document, if real, was a revelation. "Lost forever from the light bringer's crown, the jewel that contained the radiance of the Lord God, that brings light to the darkness, now sleeps in…"

Tyler leaned closer. "Go ahead, Doctor."

Innocent felt his mouth go dry. "…now sleeps in the lake that touches the sky."

Tyler nodded. "We believe this to mean Lake Victoria, and we're making the arrangements to go in through Bukoba. Tanzania's government is far more amenable to our arrival than Kenya or Uganda seem to be at the moment."

"Lake Victoria is a large body of water, Mr. Tyler."

"True, but I don't think it will be hard at all to find the jewel. Look here," Tyler said, pointing to one of the diagrams on the copy. "This we believe represents some sort of temple structure that may have been built to honor or protect the jewel. We sonar the bottom, and if we find something that looks like a building, we have a submersible to go look for it."

Innocent chuckled. "You are quite prepared."

"The consortium I represent does not like to run into the unexpected."

They continued to discuss the minutiae of the first phase of the expedition as they continued their drive to Chicago and to O'Hare International. Tyler had already seen to chartering an appropriate vessel for the nautical part of the expedition, and apparently there was a submersible vehicle that was already loaded on a Boeing 777 awaiting their arrival for departure to Nairobi, and from there to Bukoba, Tanzania. Upon arrival at the airport, they were driven to a hangar where other men, dressed in similar dark suits to the driver and his companion, were loading equipment and other, unmarked, crates onto the huge Boeing jet. A crew was fueling the plane and preparing it for takeoff, and Tyler led Innocent up the stairs attached to the entry to the plane in preparation for departure.

Inside, the plane was far different than Innocent had expected. Rather than being a standard airliner, it was outfitted more like a flying office. Wood paneling and desks, comfortable-looking chairs with safety belts being the only thing attesting to them being inside a vehicle, and multiple flat screens were among the many extravagances that adorned the airliner. Tyler eased into a seat behind one of the larger desks, and gestured for Innocent to have a seat in a comfortable-looking chair near the desk.

"We'll be taking off in fifteen minutes, Doctor," Tyler said, amiably. "Please, get comfortable. It's a long trip to Nairobi."

Innocent settled into the chair, which was as comfortable as it looked. "I'm very excited to get back into the field, Mr. Tyler."

Tyler grinned. "We're going to be spending a lot of time together, Doctor. Let's...be a little less formal, yes? 'Gerald' will suffice."

Innocent nodded. "If that is so, then 'Innocent' will be sufficient for me."

Tyler grinned a little wider. "Excellent. Now, let us put business aside for a moment, and raise a glass in honor of our grand adventure." He gestured, and one of the men in dark suits brought out two flutes of champagne, handing one to each of them. He raised his glass in salute to Innocent. "To the greatest discovery yet to be found."

Innocent smiled and raised his glass as well. "To the glory of God."

"Yes," Tyler replied. "Quite."

Ꮁᒋ0ᐱƐ�K7ᗝ⅄Ꝑ†Ꮢ∃Ꝑ∃ᒉK∃†Ꝑ

The flight was uneventful, with Innocent trying to get a quick nap in after passing London. By the time they stopped to refuel in Cairo, he had given up trying; the anxiety and excitement were far to potent. He had not been anywhere near his original home for a long time, and he knew that unrest continued from the small villages even to Kigali itself even if open warfare did not. Tribal differences were never truly settled in 1994, and to be sure, he was reticent to even return to Africa being a Christian Tutsi man. Tyler had assured his safety, though, and Innocent knew that Tyler's backers had the one thing that always seemed to handle any situation: money.

Innocent found himself wondering who this consortium was that was backing this expedition, and just what they sought to gain from finding such an obscure artifact as Lucifer's jewel. It was clear they were willing to pay just about any price to obtain it, but why? Was it for the glory of God, or was it for a more sinister purpose? Was it simply to add to a museum's collection, or for someone's personal collection? There were so many unanswered questions, but

Innocent forced himself to table them for a later day; the work had to come first, and he would get more answers when there were successes with which to barter for them.

The final leg of the flight, from Cairo to Nairobi, was a bumpy ride, with a large storm coming from seemingly nowhere over Aswan, and seeming to follow them until long past Khartoum. Eventually, the storm dissipated, and the flight smoothed out, but Innocent had been shaken enough to spend a good amount of the end of the flight in prayer, entreating the Lord for a safe landing in Nairobi. God was merciful to His child that day, for the plane landed perfectly safely in Nairobi, almost perfectly on time, and Innocent sighed with relief once he stood on solid earth once more.

The men in suits directed Innocent and Tyler to a smaller jet nearby, where they embarked for the trip to Bukoba. Innocent found himself somewhat confused by the switch, but did not question. So much about this expedition had been so unusual already, one more seemingly harmless thing would not be of consequence.

The smaller jet was as well-apportioned as the larger, if on a smaller scale. It was clearly made for shorter hops, as it lacked the office accoutrements, but there was a small bar, as well as equally comfortable-looking chairs. Tyler and

Innocent settled into the chairs and secured themselves with the safety belts.

"Best to stay secured this time," Tyler said. "I'm hearing there's some rough weather over the lake."

Innocent nodded, though his stomach did not agree. It was not unusual for there to be storms over Lake Victoria, but it felt to him that bad weather was following him for some unknown, unknowable, reason. "Good thing there is a bar, yes?"

Both men chuckled, but only Tyler seemed to be at ease. "When we're in the air, I'll pour you something."

After what felt like an interminable wait, the smaller jet finally took off from Jomo Kenyatta International, bound for Bukoba. Even with a strong thunderstorm over Lake Victoria to deal with, the flight to Bukoba was not as bad as the previous flight. Perhaps it was the single-malt that Tyler had offered Innocent, or perhaps it was just the anticipation of the work to come, but the turbulence and the distant lightning and rain didn't seem to phase Innocent in the slightest. After a somewhat pleasant six hour flight, the jet landed in Bukoba without incident, though the rain had gotten much harder, almost to the point where they might have had to reroute.

Innocent was the first off the plane, though he was not in the same hurry. The heavy rain felt good on his face, but he did not stand in it long, as he was hurried along by an impatient Tyler carrying an umbrella directly behind him. A man in a lighter suit, a man who seemed to be local, awaited them by a car as they disembarked. He grinned widely at them both and gestured for them to get in the vehicle.

"Mister Tyler, Doctor Nsabimana! Please, the rain is very bad! Come, I will take you to your hotel!" the man by the car spoke, his accent suggesting English was a second or third language.

"I did not know the consortium was sending anyone," Tyler quipped.

"Ah, our employer would not leave you in this deluge, sir," the man spoke, his voice almost a bellow. "I am Adisa Kombo, at your service, sir. Welcome to Bukoba!"

The men clambered into the waiting car, which sped off into the rainy Tanzanian night. The car was cool and comfortable on the inside, a far cry from the humid, rainy nightmare they'd experienced upon leaving the plane. Their host, this Mr. Kombo, also seemed to be a cool character, if a bit blustery, and possessed of a grin that never seemed to leave his face.

"We have arranged for you to board your ship tomorrow afternoon," Kombo spoke, after a few minutes. "The submersible has not arrived yet; there were complications in Nairobi. I am told that they will be resolved with all speed, however, and the sub will be here tomorrow morning, and will be loaded on the *Orion's Song*. Then you will be loaded on the boat and off you go! *Ha ha ha*!"

"Good. We're anxious to get out in the field," Tyler said.

It took only a few minutes to travel from the airport to the hotel, which seemed relatively comfortable, if not a five-star indulgence. The staff was pleasant, and spoke fluent English in addition to the local Swahili. Kombo buzzed around them like some sort of protective bee, making sure that the staff was cautious with the baggage and equipment, but did so in a pleasant way, his grin and jovial demeanor winning almost everyone over within minutes.

"Do not worry about gratuity, Mr. Tyler. I have it all taken care of, yes?" Kombo said, with a wide smile. He then turned to Innocent, his smile widening. "That goes for you as well, Doctor. I won't hear of you spending a penny more than necessary. Your hosts have all expenses covered, yes?"

Innocent nodded, a smile appearing on his face as well. Kombo's enthusiasm was infectious. "I would not dare offend our hosts, or our good friend Mr. Kombo."

Kombo's smile widened. "This is why you are the scholar! You understand things well! *Ha ha ha*!" He erupted into a deep belly laugh. "Now, off with you, rest and relax! I will be by tomorrow to take you to the ship. Big day tomorrow, yes? Good night!"

Innocent, for the first time since leaving Glen Allyn, felt truly good about what he was doing. The Lord was watching over him, even here in this stormy place, looking for the jewel from the crown of a fallen angel. He opened the door to his room, which was comfortable and clean, and fell upon the bed, falling asleep almost upon impact.

Chapter Three

Day broke over Bukoba, and Innocent stretched slowly, still in his clothes. The room in the hotel remained cool and comfortable, and he yawned and rubbed the sleep from his eyes as he rose and walked drowsily to the western-facing window of the room. He knew that beyond the window were wonders aplenty, such as Lake Victoria, the Serengeti, and great Mount Kilimanjaro, but all he could see from his window was another hotel, and other buildings. Such, he supposed, was the price of city life.

A knock came on his door, surprising Innocent enough to make him jump. He made his way to the door, equally surprised to find Kombo at the door, wide smile at the ready. He opened the door slowly, not sure what to expect.

"Doctor Nsabimana! Good morning!" Kombo bellowed happily. "I am here to collect you for transport to the ship, yes? Are you ready?"

Innocent looked down at his rumpled clothes, the same outfit he had worn the previous day. He wearily shrugged, and went to his duffel, pulling out an equally rumpled white bucket hat that he placed on his head. "Yes, I am ready."

Kombo laughed, a deep belly laugh. "Ah, youth. To be young again, yes? Come, the car is waiting."

Kombo shepherded Innocent to a waiting car, where Tyler was already waiting for him. Tyler had an expression of quiet patience on his face, but Innocent did not want to test it. He climbed in the car, with Kombo getting in next to the driver, another man in a dark suit. The car drove off quickly, deftly navigating the crooked streets of Bukoba. After several minutes of twists and turns, they finally arrived on the shores of Lake Victoria. There, docked at a makeshift wharf, was a large ship marked "*Orion's Song*". Several dockworkers were loading various crates and packages of a myriad of sizes aboard the vessel, while a large crane lowered what looked like a small submarine onto the deck of the *Orion's Song*. Innocent took a moment to take in all the chaos and the sheer scope of it all, and found himself speechless.

"Impressive, yes?" Tyler asked, appearing behind Innocent's shoulder. We were lucky to be able to get such a good ship on such short notice, but as they say, money greases every wheel."

"Impressive?" Innocent quipped. "Impressive is finishing paperwork on time. This…this is daunting."

Tyler clapped a hand on Innocent's shoulder. "Wait until you see the view on deck."

Together they walked up the gangway up to the main deck, and it was only then that Innocent realized just how right Tyler was; before them, in every direction, spread out the great Lake Victoria, the source of the mighty Nile River itself. The view was both awesome and terrifying, and knowing that there was a possibility of a divine relic somewhere under the waves made it all the more awesome. Innocent fell to his knees, praying silently a prayer of praise to the One who could make such a wonder.

Tyler folded his arms. "Take a moment, then join us on the bridge. We have a few things to go over before we cast off."

After a moment of silent prayer, Innocent rose from the deck and found his way to the bridge of the ship. Inside, Tyler and Kombo were speaking with a few other men, one of which, he assumed, was the captain of the vessel. Tyler spoke to one man, a world-weary looking man of light complexion and dark hair, in broken Afrikaans. Innocent's knowledge of Afrikaans was not substantial, but he knew enough to discern that the man was the captain and owner of the *Orion's Song*, and that he was unhappy with the time table.

He could also discern that Tyler did not care.

Innocent walked up to the squabbling men to be greeted by Kombo's traditional grin. "Ah, Doctor! Welcome aboard! The view is beautiful, yes?"

"It is impressive, as is this ship," Innocent said. "I'm looking forward to getting out there and starting our search."

"The sonar equipment and the submersible are ready, but it seems our captain has decided at the last moment he wants more money," Tyler grumbled. "Something about curses and other such nonsense. I told him I have to get it authorized higher up, but I am certain it will be authorized nonetheless." Tyler's phone beeped, and after a quick look at the screen, a slight grin creased his face. "There, you see?" Once more in broken Afrikaans, he informed the captain that his request was granted, and that seemed to please him.

"Batten down the hatches, yes? We are finally getting underway!" Kombo jovially bellowed.

ᚻ᚟ᛟᛜᚢ᚛ᚠᛜᛟᴧᚠᚦᛒᛖᚢᚠᚢᛒᛕᚢᚦᚠ

The weather seemed to have calmed considerably from the storms they had encountered whilst flying to Nairobi. Though the waves were present, they were no larger a swell than normal, and the *Orion's Song* cruised through them without much effort. Innocent stood on the deck looking off the bow, just taking in the view of water everywhere he could see. It was as awesome as any sight he had ever seen in his lifetime, and he once more silently praised the Lord of all, for whom but almighty God could create such splendor, such majesty, from mere water?

For several hours they had been searching the floor of the lake for anything anomalous, and though they had found many things, things like wrecked ships of various ages, cargo containers likely from smugglers ditching contraband, and the like, nothing resembling a structure was found. Innocent knew the search was going to be a long one, and he would just have to be patient. God would lead him to the fate He chose, and only that.

Tyler came out of the bridge, his face stern and irritated, and approached Innocent at the bow rail. He leaned against the rail, overlooking the massive inland sea. "Sonar reports nothing new, so we're going to move a little closer to Uganda. So far, it's bugger all, I'm afraid."

"I'm not worried," Innocent said. "If God wishes us to find something, it will be found."

Tyler chuckled. "I don't share your faith in any god or in providence, though I do miss the zeal of youth, Doctor."

Innocent recoiled in disbelief. "You do not believe? Why then do you do what you do?"

Tyler rubbed two fingers together. "It's a high-paying field. Religious conservatives love their relics."

Innocent frowned slightly. "I misunderstood your motivations, Mr. Tyler. I am not in this for any money, I do this so I may testify to the world of the reality of God."

"Opposite ends of the spectrum, I'm afraid."

"I still believe that God will decide the outcome, and if He chooses for us not to find this jewel, I am the better for seeing His great work all around us."

"I personally believe God had better make up His mind a little faster. I detest being at sea."

Innocent opened his mouth to speak but was cut off by Kombo's shout from the bridge cabin. "Doctor! Mister Tyler! You had best get up here, yes?"

Innocent's eyes widened and Tyler's frown almost instantly became a thin grin. "Looks like your God is listening after all."

The two men entered the bridge cabin to see everyone huddled around the sonar display, but they parted when

Innocent and Tyler arrived. On the screen, unbelievably, was a huge, almost geometrically perfect, square structure, with what appeared to be a series of colonnades around a large path leading to the structure. The structure was clearly damaged, but seemed to be shockingly intact for being underwater.

Tyler found his mouth agape, but quickly shook off his stunned condition. "Kombo, get on the line with Nat Geo. Find out if anyone's ever discovered this before."

"Of course, sir!" Kombo said, making his way to the comms as quickly as he could.

"Make sure we are getting as much footage of this as possible," Tyler stated, the leader starting to take over.

"Never stopped taping, sir," the young woman running the sonar responded.

"Doctor, what can you say about what we have here?"

Innocent looked at the screen, nonplussed. "I can't tell much from what we have here, but the configuration almost seems more Egyptian than sub-Saharan. That isn't possible, though; Egyptian civilization wasn't until long after the lake formed. Whoever built this was here before the Nile was."

The submersible was fueled and lowered into the waters of Lake Victoria, ready for its trip to the bottom. It was decided that Innocent, Tyler, Kombo, and the sonar operator, Kylie, would be the four to make the trip, and they all prepared themselves. They got into their wetsuits and checked the emergency gear aboard the *Lux Veritas*, for at the bottom of such a large body of water, one technical malfunction and everyone was dead. The equipment, like the crew, had to be at its best for such a journey.

They all climbed in to the vessel, and it was a tight fit, but all four managed to make it. Kombo's large frame was a bit of a squeeze, but he managed to shoehorn himself into the tight space. The hatch was sealed, and they descended into the dark of the water.

There was nothing but darkness for the majority of the trip, with the occasional fish or eel making itself seen in the cloudy water. It was an eerie experience, almost claustrophobic, and Innocent found it profoundly uncomfortable. He whispered Psalm 27 to himself to keep his mind calm, but the oppressive *nothingness* seemed to close in on him from all sides, reaching in from *everywhere*.

Then, after an almost interminable amount of time, the lights fell upon something.

Before them was a column made of some sort of stone they could not readily identify. It was smooth and greenish-black. The capital of the column was similar to that of the temple of Hathor at Denderah, though the face was not of Hathor, but some other unknown deity who defied description. The column was not parallel to the ground either, but slightly off-kilter enough to be almost troublesome to look at.

"The Lord is my light and my salvation…whom shall I fear?" Innocent whispered, trembling.

"That." Tyler also whispered.

The *Lux Veritas* ran its light further down, revealing a long causeway of the same unknown stone, flanked by colonnades of the same columns they had seen. The submersible moved slowly over the causeway until the larger structure finally came into view, and when it did, all four of them gasped in shock, for what they saw was beyond their imagining.

Before them unfolded an alien sight, a construction of an architecture that could only be described as non-human. It was built of the same unknown stone as before, but carved into irregular blocks reminiscent of the Inca structures at Sacsayhuamán. They were expertly assembled, however, into a perfectly trapezoidal building nearly ten meters in height, which would be visible from the surface of much of the lake. It was surrounded with columns identical to the colonnades along the causeway leading to the building itself, though the capitals seemed to vary, though none resembled any known deity. A massive doorway, nearly five meters in height itself, led into the structure, though one of the massive doors seemed to have fallen off over its incalculable lifetime.

The other door, still standing vigil, was of a strange, golden metal that seemed to absorb more light than it reflected. It was engraved with strange sigils that none aboard the *Lux Veritas* could decipher, but they made certain to photograph everything they could. Nothing like this had ever been discovered before, and it was important to document the find. That was the problem with underwater archaeology; most of the time the best you could hope for was images, for actual retrieval of anything was problematic at best.

"I think…I think we should try to go inside," Innocent said, finally breaking the silence that had come over the crew since the first column had been found. "I want to see what is in there."

"I don't see why not," Kombo replied from the helm. "There is more than enough room to maneuver without disturbing anything." His tone was far from jovial this time; an unusual quiet seemed to have taken him.

"See that you don't," Tyler added. "We don't know anything about what we're looking at."

Kombo slowly steered the submersible through the tight space between the massive door and the wall where the other door, now on the ground several meters away, had once hung. It was a tense squeeze, but Kombo was skilled, and they managed to slip through without incident.

Inside the structure was abyssal blackness. It was if they had passed through the event horizon of some wandering collapsed star and into the singularity without knowing. Though they shone the submersible's lamp anywhere they could, the view was the same; endless darkness. Finally, after several minutes of claustrophobic, oppressive darkness, the lamp finally fell upon an object; an altar, carved of what appeared to be red granite, inlaid with strange gemstones that glittered in the light with a malicious glimmer. Obscene runes of an alien tongue were emblazoned all over the altar, carved into the very rock. Upon the altar, resting on what appeared to be the remains of a crumbling, red cloth, was a metal box, half a meter long, also with the same alien runes carved into it. The runes seemed to be filled in with some sort of substance that appeared to be waxy or possibly have been molten at one time, for it seemed to have filled in the runes and cooled there.

"What is that?" Kylie asked, after a tense silence.

The sonar operator hired for the expedition, Kylie Ericsson was one of the best sonar technicians in the world. Her skill with even the worst of equipment had led to great discoveries worldwide, but even someone with her impressive resume had never seen something like this. Now, even with her traditional "RMS Titanic" cap pulled tightly down over her blonde hair and part of her forehead, it was easy to tell that her eyebrows were raised.

"We need to retrieve that box," Innocent added. "We must know what is in it."

"Good thing we have two manipulator arms, yes?" Kombo chirped, still quite muted.

Kombo deftly, yet slowly, moved the two manipulator arms of the submersible to surround the metal box, which to his surprise lifted off the altar quite easily. They slowly moved back out of the structure that they had begun to refer to as "the temple" and returned to the *Orion's Song*, anxious to open the box, wondering just what mysteries awaited.

Once the submersible had finally been retrieved from the water, and the crew had a chance to change and debrief with the captain, they gathered in the mess hall, Innocent bearing the mysterious box. To him it felt cool, yet almost slippery, the way an ice cube feels, but less cold. It was an odd sensation, but he felt no malice, no aura of evil. Innocent sat the box down in the middle of the assembled crew, and inhaled deeply as he pulled at the top.

Nothing happened. The box would not open.

"Perhaps you need to have your hands in a certain position," Kombo said. "Try on certain runes."

Innocent did just that; touching certain runes seemed to do nothing, but there was one rune that did seem to send a warm pulse of…something…up his arm when he touched it. He fumbled around looking for another that did the same, but there did not seem to be one.

"Oh, it is not working!" Innocent grumbled in frustration.

"Not true," Tyler interrupted. "It's working precisely as it is supposed to. You just don't know how to operate it."

Tyler placed his hand atop the box, which started to hum. He then changed the position of some of his fingers to touch certain runes, and the frequency of the hum changed, until it was inaudible, and then a loud click could be heard. Tyler removed his hand and opened the lid of the box with ease.

"The pictograms on the papyrus were the key," Tyler added." "Once I saw the runes, I knew exactly what to do."

Inside the box rested what appeared to be the largest crystal they had ever seen. It was green in color, and almost luminescent. It was cut like a gemstone, but far more than a common gemstone; there was a palpable feeling of *power* coming from this crystal. There was no good or evil in it, just sheer, raw *power*.

Innocent fell to his knees. "It…it is truly the jewel…"

Kombo unconsciously crossed himself. "Does this mean…?"

Tyler slowly nodded. "Apparently, we've got evidence that bloody *Lucifer* is real."

ᚼᚦ0ᚢƎᚨᚢ0ᚥᚠ†ᚱƎᚱƎᚾᚴƎ†ᚠ

It took several hours before the crew of the *Orion's Song* could clear their heads, but once that had happened, they met once more in the mess hall. Innocent was still somewhat in a daze, as if he had looked upon the face of God Himself. Kombo was starting to think in terms of dollars, and Tyler was starting to think in terms of skepticism. Kylie was unsure what to think at the moment, except to be wary and fearful of the massive crystal.

Innocent sat in the mess hall late that night, keeping vigil over the crystal, contemplating its mysteries. It was now secured inside a makeshift quarantine area, still resting inside of the open metal box, an eerie greenish glow now clearly illuminating the dark room. The makeshift plexiglass wall that secured the crystal did little to diminish its haunting light, and Innocent was entranced by it, entranced by what could only be the power of God almighty.

Innocent closed his eyes and began to pray, the prayer he had prayed every night for most of his life, a prayer entreating the Lord God for safety in sleep, a prayer necessitated by wars raging in his homeland, even if he could not remember them.

L'...

Innocent's eyes shot open as if electrocuted. He had heard something spoken, clear as day. There was no one around, none there but himself and the crystal. He rose, looking out the hatches that led into the mess, seeing if anyone was passing by; there was no one. He returned to the seat facing the crystal and resumed his prayer.

Vz'...

That time he knew someone had spoken, but it was impossible, for there was no one there. Either someone was playing a cruel joke, or God was speaking to him directly. Only one seemed likely, for who was *he* to be spoken to by the author of the universe?

Ratha…

Kylie slept fitfully in her bunk, a dreamless sleep that gained her little rest. In her relatively short life, she had spent a great deal of it on ships, as it went with the territory, and thus had gotten used to uncomfortable bunks, but something about this ship, this time, left her ill at ease. She'd felt eyes on her since the expedition began, being one of only two women aboard the *Orion's Song*, which was also part and parcel of her profession, but something had changed once the box had been found. Something profound had shifted, and it left her unable to rest.

Giving up, she decided to head out to the deck for some air. Pulling on a pair of leggings and a jacket, she headed out into the silent night. No one was staffing the deck, as they had decided to anchor for the night, to conserve fuel for the trip back to shore in the morning. In the distance, she could see a storm, crackling with lightning like the gods flashing lights in the clouds. It was an awesome sight, and she found herself swept up in the moment. A single tear ran down her cheek as she silently reveled in the beauty before her.

Speak the name.

So absorbed in the ecstasy of the moment, she didn't even stop to think about where the voice could have come from. She only spoke in the tiniest of whispers.

"L'vz'ratha…"

Chapter Four

The next morning, the *Orion's Song* made for port, and a certain pall hung over her crew. It was barely perceptible, but it was there; every member of the crew was quieter than before, more reserved, less jovial than they had been before the discovery of the crystal. Innocent, especially, was unusually silent, though he dismissed it as being reflective. Kylie seemed nervous, on edge, as if expecting some sort of bad news. Tyler was short tempered as always, but there seemed to be no fuse for him; anything told to him seemed to be all it took to set him off on a tirade. Kombo, however, was the most different from usual; he was sullen, silent, and rarely left his bunk unless someone specifically called for his services. Even then, he would perform his task silently, and with no expression on his face, and leave as soon as his task was done, returning to his bunk.

Innocent was concerned as to the sudden change in behavior, and thought it best to speak with his fellows before they departed for the next leg of the expedition, wherever that might be. Though he knew Tyler was in an extraordinarily bad mood, he knew Tyler was also the only one who knew anything about the next destination, so it made sense, even if unpleasant.

He knocked on the hatch to Tyler's berth, and received a curt greeting. "Enter!"

"Mr. Tyler, I wanted to talk to you about…"

Tyler interrupted with wrathful vigor. "Get to it!"

Innocent recoiled in surprise, but continued. "Our next destination. Are you at liberty to discuss where we are going?"

Tyler closed his eyes and inhaled deeply. "I'm sorry, Doctor Nsabimana. I seem to be a little on edge since…our discovery. Please forgive my rudeness."

"It is forgiven."

"As for where we are going," Tyler continued, "we are not completely sure. The text says that 'the fall will be made manifest through the eye of Lucifer', which we assumed to mean the jewel, but as you've seen, there's no evident location. I searched the box for anything else, a false panel, anything…but there was nothing but the crystal."

"Not true," Innocent said. "There are the runes on the box. We may not understand them, but I think they may be exactly what we are looking for."

"How, though?"

No sooner had Tyler spoken then a sudden, jarring shock hit the ship with such force that everyone seemed to be thrown three feet to their left. The power flickered on and off for a few seconds and shouts in Swahili and Afrikaans could be heard in the bowels of the vessel as the engineers tried to figure out what had happened. Tyler and Innocent had been thrown to the deck hard, but managed to pull themselves back to their feet quickly. They ran as fast as they could to the bridge, where the others had congregated as well, all in a panic state, wondering just what had happened. Kylie was at her sonar station, looking for any objects that may have drifted into their path, but saw nothing.

"What happened?" Tyler demanded of the captain. The captain screamed back at him in Afrikaans, eyes wide with terror.

Innocent looked to Tyler, confused. "What did he say?"

Tyler, equally confused, spoke slowly. "He said…he said that just for a second…a crack in the air opened and *something* grabbed the ship, and that as soon as we get to port we are to get off his ship and never return."

Kombo scoffed. "Nonsense. He's been drinking. I can smell cheap whiskey on him from here."

Tyler spoke once more in Afrikaans to the captain, who responded once more in a fury. "He says he *has* been drinking, but not so much that he'd be seeing things, never mind that you'd be feeling them."

"Something happened," Kylie added, "but I can't find anything in sonar range that might have hit us. Still, I have trouble buying that something came out of thin air and grabbed us."

"Let's just get to port and figure it out from there," Tyler said, with finality. Everyone seemed to agree, and dispersed from the bridge, but everyone still had a certain reticence about what they believed about what had just happened. With all the strangeness that had already taken place, was something blinking into existence and grabbing the ship *really* so weird?

ᎤᏞ0ᏉꞜᏉ0ᎷꞠᛏᏒᎧꞠᎧᏔᏦᎧᛏꞠ

The *Orion's Song* finally made it to port, much to the relief of all, with no further incident. Innocent and Kombo saw to the packaging of the crystal, which was placed back into the runed metal box, and then crated. It would be kept as unassuming as possible, considering the ramifications of the artifact on society, until more was known about its composition and history. They could not just announce that they had found a relic verifying the existence of Satan; there were procedures that had to be followed.

Tyler had decided to move operations to Geneva, where more scientific (and skeptical) eyes could examine the artifact. In the meantime, he had arranged to have Innocent, Kombo, and Kylie put up at The Woodward, as they would still be needed for the next phase of the expedition, but while analysis of the crystal was going on, there wasn't much they could do. Innocent was overwhelmed at the sheer scale of the massive hotel, as he was not accustomed to luxury of any sort, much less on such a grand scale as that. Kylie and Kombo, on the other hand, were more than pleased to relax in such plush quarters; after the tight squeeze of the *Orion's Song* and the strange goings-on of late, some rest in such luxurious quarters was most welcome.

Kombo, Kylie, and Innocent retired to their rooms, which were all luxurious suites, after one final meeting with Tyler and another gentleman identifying himself as "Matthews" that had met the crew upon their arrival in Geneva. All indulged in a relaxing shower, and prepared themselves for bed, ready to put the insanity of the last couple days behind them.

It was shortly after three A.M. when Kylie was awakened by a sudden noise in her room, something that sounded like some large object being dragged. Her eyes shot open in terror and alertness as she slowly moved her arm towards her travel bag, where the .38 was kept that she always had on hand just in case. The sound came from near the bathroom, which was a good five meters or so from her king-size bed. She moved slowly, slowly, not wanting to catch the attention of whatever it was that was making the noise, creeping closer to her gun.

Just as she was about to reach the bag, *something* grabbed her arm with horrible force, and she tried to scream. *Something* clapped down over her mouth, something wet and powerful, but not a human hand. It was something else, something terrible. She could feel its fetid breath on her as it tried to shift its bulk onto her body. She fought with all of her might, but the thing was too strong, and it managed to climb atop her, wrapping some sort of horrific appendages around her. She screamed a muffled scream of terror as she resisted with her every ounce of strength, but it was useless. She could hear a terrible growl inches from her face, and feel some vile fluid drip onto her as she caught the slightest glimpse of teeth, sharp and jagged, moving towards her.

"Kylie?" Kombo's voice came from outside of her room's door after a polite knock. "Kylie, are you in there?"

Upon hearing the sound of the voice, the horrible thing seemed to dash away into the shadows. Kylie finally was able to scream, and dashed for the door as she did, letting Kombo enter. She fell into his arms, weakly sobbing.

"What happened?" Kombo asked, clearly worried.

"Something…*something* attacked me, but you scared it off."

"We are all still on edge after that…that thing was found," Kombo muttered. "Come, you stay in my room tonight. I will take the sofa."

"Thank you," Kylie replied. "I don't want to be alone."

The door shut behind them, but eyes watched them still, eyes that saw more than they knew.

ꝄΓΟꝸϿ☦ꝸΟΛꞆ†ꝛϿꞆϿꞆꝂϿ†Ꞇ

Innocent was lying in his bed, unable to sleep. He had said many prayers, for just about everything imaginable, but still his soul was not at peace. There was an unshakeable feeling of being watched, being *observed*, and it gnawed at his consciousness. There was nothing in his room out of the ordinary; he'd left a light on because he was uncomfortable being in an unfamiliar environment and in the pitch black of the hotel room. He was sure many a traveler found the darkness and silence soothing. On this night, he found them utterly terrifying.

Innocent slid out of the massive, soft bed and grabbed his duffel, rummaging through it briefly, and pulling out a small prescription bottle. It was mostly secret that he suffered from severe anxiety, and it was completely secret that he took clonazepam to counteract it. He flipped open the bottle and dumped a few pills into his hand, which he swallowed dry. He had little choice but to keep this secret, for if word got out that he was taking medication for a mental condition, his detractors would destroy his reputation even more than they already had, and there would be no grants, no digs, no discoveries ever again. He would be disgraced in his field, and would be lucky if he was allowed to dig in a sandbox.

No, he would keep it to himself and his doctor, and everything would work out just fine, especially once the discovery of the temple and the crystal were made public. He would be heralded as a hero of the field, and the book rights alone would make him a rich man. Of course, it was all for the glory of God first and foremost, but surely the Lord wouldn't mind him benefitting as well, would He?

The clonazepam hit his system quickly, and he felt his mind slow down to a crawl, and he sighed with relief. He crawled back into bed and curled up comfortably, drifting off into sleep at last.

That is, until he awoke to the sensation of someone smacking him across the arm with what felt like a stick.

He opened his eyes, and found himself in a white room, brightly lit and unfurnished, except for a plain, wooden chair that he was tied to. He was nude, but the rope that bound him seemed to cover the naughty parts. In the room with him was a tall woman, in full dominatrix gear, holding a black riding crop. She had multi-colored dreadlocks that seemed all the more shocking against her pale skin. She wore dark, round sunglasses and dark makeup. She had a wicked sneer on her face.

Innocent concluded that he must be having some sort of bizarre nightmare, albeit one unlike any he'd ever had. Sexually charged dreams were not something he often had. He decided it was best to play along, and see how everything unfolded; perhaps he could glean some meaning from it at that point.

"Hello, *Herr Doktor*," the woman said, smirking. "Do you know who I am?"

"No, I'm afraid I do not," Innocent replied.

The woman seemed to grin evilly at his response, and placed the far end of her crop under his chin, lifting his head up to meet her gaze, which felt like ice, even behind those dark lenses. "My name is Mandy, but you may call me Mistress."

"If you wish," he replied.

A frown immediately crossed her face and she lashed out with the crop, smacking him across the chest. "'Yes, Mistress' is all you need say right now."

"Yes, Mistress," he said, wincing in pain. His heart began to pound out of control, as if in the beginning of a panic attack.

"Much better, worm," Mandy said. "Now, what to do with you…"

Mandy moved uncomfortably close to his body, her hands running along his thighs, giving him thoughts he actively fought against having. She ran her tongue from just above his navel up to his collarbone, feeling his shivers of alternating delight and disgust.

"Why fight it?" Mandy shouted at him up close. "Do you really think God cares? Do you really think that God exists? Your generic little God with no name?" She tore away her leathers to reveal her own nude body and she climbed atop Innocent's lap, reaching her hand underneath the rope in order to release his penis for her own gratification. She looked him in the eyes and smiled. "Say the name. SAY IT!"

Innocent shot up in his bed almost as fast as his erection and screamed.

"L'VZ'RATHA!"

Across the city, at the St. Pierre Laboratories, a full complement of scientific staff as well as Tyler and Matthews were working on analyzing the crystal. They had noticed odd fluctuations in its energy field around three A.M., though they were not sure what the significance of the fluctuations was. Another team was in a different lab, attempting to analyze and decode the metal box in which the crystal had been found. Both teams had been working around the clock, with staggered breaks, trying desperately to verify something, *anything*, about the artifacts.

Matthews, well behind the glass barrier erected to contain the crystal, looked upon the enigmatic artifact with a scowl. Matthews was considerably younger than Tyler, with jet-black hair and a pencil-thin beard to match. He was immaculately groomed, even for having gone two days without sleep, and only his bloodshot eyes told the tale. "What if we're looking at this the wrong way?" he posited suddenly, almost startling Tyler with his deep baritone.

"How do you mean?" Tyler replied.

"We've been proceeding on the assumption that the crystal contains the solution, but what if it doesn't? What if the crystal is only the key to obtaining the solution?"

"Fine, fine, but what then will give us the solution?"

"Clearly, Mr. Tyler, you haven't seen 'Hellraiser'," Matthews chided. "The box. The runes on the box have *got* to mean *something*, right? I bet you that the crystal somehow will tell us."

"Very well then, how?" Tyler expectantly asked. "Our employers aren't patient men."

"I don't know," Matthews sighed. "but I *will* figure it out."

⸸⌐O⅄Ǝ⫟⅄OɅ⅁⸸ⱶⱶƷ⅁ƷꞀⰍƷ⫟⅁

The next morning came, and the members of the team staying at The Woodward rose from fitful and miserable sleep.

The troubling events of the previous night had left all three of them uneasy and nervous. Kylie was left especially shaken, constantly looking over her shoulder for a beast that she had never seen. Innocent spent a good portion of the morning in prayer, worried that such a horrible dream meant that there was some diabolical taint on his soul, one that only the forgiveness of Christ could ameliorate. Eventually he felt his contrition sufficient, and ordered tea and toast from room service, still shaken by the dream of the woman he'd never met, this terrible woman named "Mandy"

Kombo, on the other hand, had ordered a small feast, justifying it with not knowing what was going to come next throughout the day. Kylie, agreeing that just about anything was possible at that point, picked at the feast a bit, but found it difficult to eat when she was still so terrified. She was afraid the creature would return, and was also somewhat repulsed at the way Kombo ate.

Suddenly, the phone in Kombo's room rang, making both of them jump in surprise. Kombo quickly answered, curious as to what was going on.

"Hello?"

Matthews spoke with trepidation on the other end. "Mr. Kombo, would you please get the others and join us at the lab as soon as you can?"

Kombo spoke quietly. "Of course." He hung up the phone, and looked at Kylie, "They want us at the lab."

Kylie's eyes widened, for she feared what it could be that required their presence near the crystal.

Chapter Five

The third angel blew his trumpet, and a great star fell from heaven, blazing like a torch, and it fell on a third of the rivers and on the springs of water. The name of the star is Wormwood. A third of the waters became wormwood, and many died from the water, because it was made bitter.

The Revelation of St. John 8:10-11

The car pulled up to the laboratory building, and the three members of the crew exited without a word. A terrible fear, palpable around them, hung in the air as they entered the building, escorted by security personnel. They were led through a labyrinth of doors, none of which told what lay behind them; only a three-digit number bespoke of what might lay beyond that particular portal. Some had people in lab coats coming and going, others did not open as they passed. The laboratory in general seemed a very busy place, but none seemed as busy as the area they were led to, the one assigned to crack the mystery of the crystal and its container.

As Innocent, Kombo, and Kylie were finally escorted into the lab area with the crystal, they were blown away at the sight of a dozen or more people in the same white coats hard at work at various monitors and stations, all trying to penetrate the mysteries of the two objects they had found at the bottom of Lake Victoria. From one corner of the room, Innocent could see the familiar greenish glow of the crystal, and he felt himself drawn to it. He walked slowly towards the crystal, and as he did, an odd vibration started to resonate throughout the room. The scientists on hand started to dash to various monitoring stations, trying to analyze the vibration, but none could even detect it on any instrument, though everyone could feel it. Then, as quickly as it had come, it ceased, and everyone stared at Innocent, who seemed entranced by the crystal.

After several moments of silence, Innocent spoke, slowly, as if given a great revelation. "It is so simple. The crystal sees the way. It is the eye, the seraph's eye, the way to find the fall."

Tyler, exhausted and frustrated from a long night of work, walked up to Innocent, a scowl on his face. "What are you talking about?"

Innocent turned, a smile on his face. "She told me. The priestess told me. It is the eye."

Matthews turned to one of the scientists, one who held some sort of instrument. "Is there any sort of appreciable radiation coming from the crystal?"

The scientist shook his head. "No sir, there's nothing but normal background."

Matthews opened the containment chamber and took hold of the crystal. The glow vanished immediately, and the beatific look on Innocent's face vanished as well. He hung his head in embarrassment and said nothing more. Matthews, however, looked more determined than ever, and made a beeline for the box that had held the crystal. With resolve, albeit with great trepidation as well, he raised the crystal to his eyes and peered through it at the box.

A moment passed, then another, and then Matthews gasped. "God in Heaven, it works."

Tyler stormed over to Matthews and snatched the crystal from his hands. "Let me see that!" He too raised the crystal to his eyes, and his mouth fell agape. "My God…he's right. It…it's right there…"

Before them, on the box that had been so incomprehensible, was now dozens of lines of cuneiform script. The crystal somehow interpreted the bizarre runes on the box into something they could understand…or more specifically, something Innocent could understand.

Tyler waved for Innocent to join them, and proffered the crystal to him. Innocent approached slowly, still remembering the dream from the night before, the horrors the woman, this "priestess", had inflicted on him, the terrible sins he'd committed in his mind thinking about her as she violated him, and that somehow her voice had spoken to him through the crystal, but now they needed him to see what the eye saw.

Innocent slowly, gingerly accepted the crystal, looking at it, turning it in his hands. It filled him with equal measures of dread and excitement as he held it, for this was the key to everything he'd ever dreamed of, but it was also connected somehow to this "Mandy", and already she had attempted to corrupt him. He had managed to cling to his faith thus far, but he suspected she was not done tempting him. Still, he had to do what must be done, and he lifted the crystal to his eyes.

The cuneiform script was revealed to him, and he smiled. "It's Sumerian. You might want to write this down, or record it."

Tyler scoffed. "We've never stopped recording everything, Dr. Nsabimana. Go ahead."

Innocent coughed uncomfortably. "'One third of Heaven, one full measure of the Hosts of the Lord stood with Lucifer as he denied the will of El, who is called Yah. For this, they were cast out of…' Now that's odd."

Matthews sharply turned to look straight at Innocent. "What's odd?"

Innocent pointed to the box that had contained the crystal. "The word that comes next means 'ship' or 'sailboat', but that doesn't make any sense. 'For this, they were cast out of the ship. They were banished to…Tiama't?' What is this?"

Tyler looked both anxious and expectant. "Is that it?"

Innocent looked quite disturbed. "No. There is more, but…it is absurd!"

Tyler began to turn red. "Read it!" he hissed.

Innocent continued, though through serious misgivings. "They were banished to Tiama't, and forever branded Anu'naki in the sight of El who is Yah. It then came that Tiama't came to the world of men, and the Anu'naki came to rule over Ur and Uruk, and Lucifer sat upon a throne of light in Ur.'"

A horrible silence filled the room, and Innocent carefully set the crystal down and backed away as if it were poisonous. No one wanted to speak, and yet everyone wanted to talk, for the interpretation of the box text was as ludicrous and yet horrific as it could have possibly been.

Tyler cleared his throat, taking the initiative to speak first. "So it's Ur we must go to."

Innocent shook his head. "I can have no part of this nonsense."

It was then Matthews' turn to scoff. "Excuse me?"

"I cannot be part of this blasphemy any longer. You are trying to tell me that Lucifer and the angels are *aliens*? It is blasphemous and I cannot be part of it."

"You can and *will*," Tyler growled, "because you have come this far, and there can be *no* turning back now! You want to know your god? *THIS* is the way to do it."

Innocent recoiled from the rebuff. "Very well, but understand that I do this under protest."

"Noted," Tyler hissed.

Matthews lifted the crystal and placed it back in its containment area, and immediately it began to glow once more, though this time the glow was a pale white, far dimmer than it had been.

Innocent slowly made his way back to his room once they arrived back at The Woodward. He had remained in sullen silence the entire trip back from the St. Pierre laboratory, and the others traveling with him were quite concerned, trying to ease his foul mood, to no avail. Any attempt to engage him in conversation was met with stern rebuff, and once the car returned to The Woodward, he opened the door quickly and disembarked without a word, disappearing into the hotel with alacrity.

Once back in his room, Innocent locked the door behind him and immediately fell to his knees by his bedside, entreating the Lord for forgiveness for the unforgiveable crime of blasphemy. In his eyes, the very existence of the crystal and its message of sacrilegious history was offensive to him as a Christian, and must therefore be offensive to God. He shared in the responsibility for finding the crystal, and therefore was accountable for it.

After a while, a tentative knock was heard at his door, breaking his reverie. Much to his chagrin, he stood, his legs aching from being folded underneath him for so long. He stood at the door, his hand on the lock and his eyes closed, not wanting to open it for several seconds, hoping that whoever it was wasn't going to knock again. Unfortunately for him, they did knock again a few seconds later, and he sighed quietly as he unlatched the door to open it. Standing outside, looking concerned, was Kylie, the sonar operator.

Remembering his manners, Innocent gestured for her to enter. "Please…come in."

Kylie walked in, looking around warily, as if she were being followed. "Sorry. It's like everywhere I go, I feel like someone's watching me. Someone bad."

Innocent nodded, definitely sharing in her paranoia. "It is fine. I have had my suspicions since this expedition began."

"May I sit for a moment?" Kylie asked, seeming weary.

"Please," replied Innocent.

"Thanks," Kylie said, a small bit of cheer returning to her voice. Innocent had noticed that she normally had a certain cheerfulness that she tried to mask with a measure of grouchiness, and he suspected deep down she was, or had been, an overly positive person. "I doubt I'll be doing much sleeping tonight."

Innocent sat down on the sofa across from the chair where Kylie sat, crossing his legs in a very conservative pose.

"I, myself, am still trying to reconcile what we discovered with what I believe, and the two are just not meshing well."

"So?" Kylie inquisitively asked.

"So, what they are trying to tell me is that even though I have seen *indisputable* evidence that the world is around six thousand years old and that God and Christ are *real* and very much *alive*, a shiny *rock* we found underwater is somehow proof that all of that is *wrong*. As a Christian and as an archaeologist, I have to question this."

A beat of silence passed, and then Kylie awkwardly giggled. "Silly," she said, teasingly. "The world is more like *four billion* years old, and as for God, I guess that's a matter of faith."

Innocent raised an eyebrow. "Prove that!"

"Prove yours!"

An awkward moment passed, and then both erupted into raucous laughter. "I left my proof in my other pants," Innocent finally said when he could catch his breath.

"A shame," Kylie said once her laughter died down sufficiently to speak. "I guess you'll have to rid yourself of those."

Innocent went slack-jawed for a moment, but never took his eyes off of Kylie. He could not understand where this conversation was going. Was she flirting with him? Did she have carnal intent?

More importantly, did he?

Innocent had found himself thinking such impure thoughts about women as he was thinking about Kylie far more often since the disturbing dream about the woman named Mandy, and speaking that name, that horrific name…but what was that name? Who did it invoke? Or what? There were so many questions he had to answer, but right now there was a more immediate concern; a lovely woman sending out what Innocent perceived as very clear signals.

It's not that Christians eschew sexuality, it's just standard practice to wait until marriage, and Innocent was married to his work. He had been quite happy with his life being the way it was until he had come on this terrifying expedition with its damnable rock and blasphemous Sumerian text. However, it had lead him to a very unexpected situation, one where he had to make a choice, one that was unpleasant and yet quite pleasant at the same time.

"Innocent?" Kylie interrupted. "Are you alright?"

He shook off his reverie and smiled at Kylie. He didn't know what was going to happen, but he would just decide as the choices were put before him. To obsess is to drive one mad. "Yes, I am fine, just…thinking about everything that has gone on."

"Yeah, me too," she replied. "like where that crystal could have come from. I've never seen anything like it."

"I'm no geologist, but I can tell you it's no stone I have ever seen. The whole temple complex was built of minerals that were unfamiliar to me."

"Do you think," she said, a slight blush falling over her pale skin, "there's a chance…don't laugh…that maybe it's aliens?"

Innocent grinned but no laugh escaped his lips. "I've seen many strange things, but they all turned out to be made by human hands. Just because we don't understand it doesn't make it alien. The pyramids of Giza were not created by alien anti-gravity beams, Stonehenge was not made by Merlin's sorcery, and the Carnac stones were not made by giants, and yet we have no idea how any of them were constructed, do we?"

Kylie playfully giggled. "No, we don't."

Kylie slowly rose from the chair where she sat and slid down next to Innocent on the sofa, laying her head on his shoulder. "I don't know why, but I feel so much safer here…with you."

Innocent felt something stirring inside of him, something he had rarely felt within his lifetime, and certainly had rarely felt since his commitment to Christ: desire. White hot desire for Kylie started to well up within him, rising from the soles of his feet to the very crown of his head. He unconsciously stroked her cheek with his hand. "You are safe."

Kylie raised her head to look him in his deep brown eyes, and within them she could see a man in turmoil. "I…I could go…"

A single second, one that felt like eternity passed, and then his hand took her around the waist. "No."

Kylie pressed herself against him and kissed him passionately, and he responded in kind, their hands exploring each other manically, as if searching for each other's most secret truths. Kylie tore the buttons off of his Oxford shirt as she tore it open, revealing his lean, muscular chest. She ran her hands along his abdominal muscles as they continued to kiss, and he returned the favor by pulling her top off over her head and undid her bra as quickly as he could, fumbling with the clasp in back due to a lack of practice. Finally removing the offending garment, he set her breasts free for his hands to explore, touching each part as slowly as he could, as if learning the structure by touch alone.

They remained on the sofa, kissing and touching each other's bare skin for several minutes, but then Kylie rose, taking Innocent's hand and leading him to his king-size bed. She unfastened her jeans, pulling both those and her panties down, revealing her nude body *in toto*, and biding him to do the same. He followed suit, releasing a penis that had become quite erect by this point, craving the insertion and release. Kylie took him by the hands and led him down onto the bed, spreading her legs wide and inviting him in.

Innocent gently entered her, slowly at first, not wanting to hurt her, but began to gain speed and power after he'd had a chance to feel her out more. She moaned with ecstasy as he thrust harder and harder, and for several minutes he kept up a good rhythm, bringing her to the edge and beyond.

"Oh, *FUCK*…oh god, yes…come inside me, please…" Kylie said.

It wasn't long before Innocent honored her request, finally reaching orgasm himself, feeling the warm release within her, and he stopped moving for a moment, just lingering in the moment.

Kylie panted, opened her eyes, and smiled. "Thanks."

Suddenly, a large, spiky appendage of some sort came out of nowhere and smashed into Innocent's side, knocking him off the bed, causing him to fall screaming to the floor. He was less hurt than just knocked off-balance, and quickly clambered to his feet, turning back to face the bed, where Kylie had been.

Now, a horror lay, coiled like some sort of serpent. It still had some of Kylie's features, especially around the face, which were horrifyingly distorted and twisted into some sort of horrific visage of nightmare. Four meaty tentacles lined with sharp barbs protruded from the sides of the beast. Razor fangs lined the mouth of the creature, which dripped with saliva that was just a little too viscous to be healthy. It leapt from the bed at him, flailing the tentacles as it flew by, but Innocent managed to dodge out of the way, ducking under the bed. The creature flew past, smashing through the door leading into the rest of the hotel, and disappearing down a corridor.

Innocent immediately threw some clothes and made a dash for Kylie's room, a sinking feeling in the pit of his stomach. Sure enough, when he got there, the door was open. He walked in to find Kylie on her bed with a book open, her head nearly torn off at the neck by forces unknown. He silently fell to his knees at the foot of her bed, whispering a prayer to the Lord, hoping that God would forgive his indiscretion with that…thing.

"It's a shame about Kylie," a familiar voice whispered behind him, "but the Ven escaped containment. Now we have to take…more severe measures."

Innocent moved to turn around but before he could, something blunt hit him in the head and the world became black as night and silent as death.

<h1 style="text-align:center">Chapter Six</h1>

Then one of the seven angels who had the seven bowls came and said to me, 'Come, I will show you the judgment of the great prostitute who is seated on many waters, with whom the kings of the earth have committed sexual immorality, and with the wine of whose sexual immorality the dwellers on earth have become drunk.' And he carried me away in the Spirit into a wilderness, and I saw a woman sitting on a scarlet beast that was full of blasphemous names, and it had seven heads and ten horns. The woman was arrayed in purple and scarlet, and adorned with gold and jewels and pearls, holding in her hand a golden cup full of abominations and the impurities of her sexual immorality. And on her forehead was written a name of mystery: 'Babylon the great, mother of prostitutes and of earth's abominations'

-The Revelation of St. John 17:1-5

Innocent awoke to a massive headache and the realization that he was bound and in a dark chamber…somewhere. There was no indication as to where, no windows, and no one around him to give him any clues as to why he was where he was, or who had put him here. He tugged on his hands, securely fastened behind him, and heard the rattle of chains. Whoever had put him here had intended for him to remain.

As for the voice that had spoken before he was knocked out, it had been passingly familiar. It had almost sounded like Matthews, but why would Matthews knock him out and imprison him? And what was a Ven? Was it the horrible Kylie-*thing* that had seduced him to sexual immorality? It was one thing to sin with someone *human*, but with that terrible *thing*…the sin felt almost multiplied.

Pushing himself to a seated position with his elbow, Innocent looked around the chamber he was in. It was nondescript; blank walls, a bulkhead door or hatch, implying that he was on some sort of sea vessel. There was no cot or anything implying that this was intended to keep prisoners, so Innocent reasoned his abduction was an emergency act. His captors had no choice but to take him, but why? Was the creature something he was not meant to see? What did this have to do with the expedition?

So many questions, but so few answers, and Innocent Nsabimana was naturally someone who looked for answers, even if he had to dig for them.

The hatch opened shortly after Innocent managed to sit upright, and as he had suspected, Matthews walked into his makeshift cell, looking unhappy in the extreme. He looked down at Innocent with a scowl. "Well, Dr. Nsabimana, it looks like the expedition has changed somewhat, thanks in part to you."

"What is going on here?" Innocent demanded.

"I doubt you would actually want to know, but I will tell you that we're currently in one of our…organization's…installations, awaiting orders from higher up as to what to do with you. We're making plans, and we're waiting to see if those include you or not."

"Organization? What are you talking about?"

Matthews smirked. "Again, I doubt you'd want to know the answer to that," he said, scoffing.

A radio on Matthews' hip crackled to life, and a voice came through. "Matthews, this is Dargaard. Bring our guest to my office. It's been decided he's coming."

Matthews grabbed the radio and pressed the transmit button. "Yes, Mr. Dargaard." Matthews grabbed a keyring from his pocket and unlocked the chain that connected

Innocent to the wall, but left his arms restrained. He helped Innocent to his feet. “Let’s go, Doctor.”

“Where am I going?” Innocent asked.

“To get some of your questions answered, but as I said, you are not going to like the answers.”

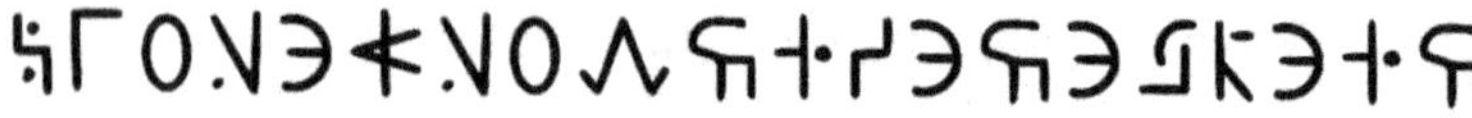

Matthews led Innocent through a labyrinth of dark corridors and tunnels that seemed to go on forever, but finally arrived at what looked like some sort of command center, with several computer terminals being manned by technicians with odd headsets that covered one eye and both ears. The screens didn’t display anything he could recognize. Matthews led him into an office just off the command center, where a man awaited them behind a massive ebony desk. The man was as white as death’s passing, with pale blond hair, long and pulled back into a neat tail behind him. He was painfully thin and gaunt, almost emaciated, and his eyes almost seemed too bloodshot to be healthy. Matthews forced Innocent down into one of the chairs in front of the desk.

“Doctor Nsabimana, I welcome you to our installation,” the thin man spoke, in a voice far too deep for his frail body. The voice seemed to well up from a dank cave or endless pit in the earth. "I am Henrik Dargaard, and I am the administrator of this facility."

"Why am I here?" Innocent demanded.

Dargaard's mouth became a snarl of thinly veiled wrath, and his bloodshot eyes narrowed. "I recommend that you control yourself. Decorum counts for a lot with me. The better you behave, the more I may be willing to share with you."

Innocent closed his eyes and breathed. "I…I am sorry."

Though his expression changed very little, it still changed enough to suggest that Dargaard was pleased, or at least, amused with Innocent's acquiescence. "There, you see? Much better. Now, as I said, I am the administrator of this facility. The reason for your…being brought here…is because you were…intimate…with one of the Ven that escaped containment here. We needed to make sure you were not infected by the creature, i.e. a slow, painful transformation into one of them. By the way, Doctor, you were not. Congratulations, I suppose."

Innocent recoiled in horror at the thought of his actions of the past few days. "I…I did not know…"

"No, you didn't," Dargaard said with a smirk. "No one
does. That is how they hunt. They take genetic samples from
prior victims and use them to mimic their prey well enough
to…seduce future prey enough to either consume them or
infect them. That is what the Ven do. In your case, it
consumed what I imagine was a healthy dose of genetic
material."

Burning with shame, Innocent merely let his head hang
slightly, avoiding Dargaard's all-seeing gaze. "Where did the
Ven come from?"

"The Ven, dear Doctor," Dargaard wheezed, "come
from exactly where you are going; the point of impact. The
very place where the Anu'naki arrived on this planet."

Dargaard began to cough heavily, and covered his
mouth with a grey handkerchief. Innocent thought he could
see small droplets of blood as Dargaard took the cloth away
from his face. He looked almost embarrassed as he composed
himself, even though Innocent tried hard to pretend as if he
hadn't noticed.

"Cancer, Doctor Nsabimana, is the great equalizer, I
fear. It cares not who it devours: rich, poor, white, black,
small, mighty." Dargaard mopped at the corners of his mouth.
"Fortunately for me, my employer allows me to do my job as

long as I am able. Thus I offer you the same courtesy. You still have use to us, so you still may work as long as you are useful." Dargaard's expression did not change; he almost seemed contrite.

"Very well," Innocent said. "But if I may, could I ask a couple of questions?"

Dargaard's mouth twisted into what might have been called a grin. "You may ask."

"Who is it you all work for?"

Dargaard twisted his mouth into a grin once more. "I work for the Church, of course."

"I find that highly unlikely that you work for the Vatican."

Sounding much like some sort of wheezy cough, a sound that may have been a laugh escaped Dargaard's throat, hard enough that he mopped his mouth once more with the now-crimson-stained handkerchief. "I did not say which Church I worked for, Doctor. There are a great many out there, but there is only one you need concern yourself with, and it is most assuredly not based in Rome."

"I believe I understand," Innocent said, slowly nodding his comprehension. "I just have one more question for you, Mr. Dargaard. Who is L'vz'ratha?"

Dargaard's eyes widened at the sound of the name, as if he were greatly surprised to hear it spoken. "How…how do you know that name?"

"I heard it spoken in a dream."

Dargaard scowled immediately, as if something had gone horribly, terribly awry. "Come with me."

ᎪᏱ0ᏉƎ₭Ꮩ0ᎪᎮ†ᏝƎᎮƎᏗᏦƎ†Ꭾ

Innocent was led to a larger area, before a set of massive metal doors. The doors appeared to be forged from the same metal as the temple beneath the waters of Lake Victoria, but the luster and brilliance of the green had gone out of them long ago, leaving more of a dull greenish sheen. He looked up at the massive doors in awe, but also in confusion. He could not understand why these were here, or why he had been brought to them.

The man he had come to know as Matthews was there, waiting for their arrival, and bowed slightly in deference to Dargaard as they approached. "Sir."

"She has called this one," Dargaard wheezed. "Open the sanctuary."

Matthews nodded and pulled on the large, circular metal pulls on the doors, and they slowly swung open with a colossal creak. Innocent could see nothing inside but darkness, save for the flickering light of a few candles. Something about this place filled him with terror; some primal instinct bade him flee from the hungering dark within, and yet paralyzed him with dread at the same time. No part of him, not even his curiosity, wanted to enter what he sensed to be a most unholy place.

Dargaard pushed Innocent lightly on the back towards the devouring maw of darkness. "You must go alone to be judged. She has called only you."

"Who has called me? What do you mean 'judge' me?"

Dargaard stood stone still. "I cannot say more. You must go inside."

Terrified, Innocent slowly turned towards the icy darkness that loomed before him. He took a few small, tentative steps, and the shadows seemed to swirl around him, imprisoning him in that unholy dark. As he traveled further in, even breathing seemed to be harder, as if something was crushing his chest. Fear unlike any he'd ever known rampaged through his mind, ripping all reason apart.

Suddenly, the shadows parted, revealing a plain, granite altar, upon which a glass decanter sat. Inside the decanter appeared to be wine of some sort, an odd pale red. There was no statuary, no tome of secrets, no blood-stained sacrificial blade, and yet Innocent felt terror beyond words even at such a plain sight. He felt a sense of utter *wrongness* that he could not categorize, for reason had left him as he'd entered the penumbra.

"Your god is a lie, you know," a familiar voice spoke from somewhere around him. "He doesn't exist. He never existed."

From the darkness stepped a woman, a very familiar woman; pale skin, a cascade of dreadlocks tied back behind her. She wore some sort of dark robe-like garment, but where her skin was exposed, brilliant tattoos could be seen. She smiled almost beatifically, her dark purple eyes locked with Innocent's. Somehow, the woman who had seduced and raped him in his dreams stood before him now; Mandy was manifest.

"I do not hear the lies of the deceiver!" Innocent shouted, his cries echoing inside the chamber.

Mandy merely laughed. "I do not deceive you. Look around you, Innocent. Look at *me*. You dreamt of me, and I appeared to you. You knew the name of the Mother though you had never spoken it before. These are facts, Innocent."

"No!" screamed Innocent. "Christ is my salvation!"

Mandy moved, too quickly for a human to move, right in Innocent's face, her nose almost touching his. "No! Surrender is your salvation! Stop fighting! Say the name! Call her name!"

"I…I won't…the name of Christ will…"

"Do nothing," Mandy taunted. "Christ was little more than an excuse for Europeans to butcher Muslims and deprive minorities of their rights because of 'religious freedoms', and you know it." She took a step back, and smiled once more, shrugging her garment a little off of one shoulder. "There *is* a better way, though. Give in, Innocent. Renounce the false god of violence and hate and call the Mother's name. You could even have *me* if you like. Whenever you like. Would that please you? She would reward you with endless pleasures, Innocent."

Innocent fell to his knees, broken. He knew all that Mandy had said was true. He had seen the rampant homophobia and transphobia veiled in the name of

Christianity, and he had done nothing. He had seen hate groups grow strong by declaring themselves a religion and, he had done nothing. He had seen lies and betrayal become commonplace and he had done nothing. He had even seen men he looked up to waste tax money building an ark, and for what?

What did it mean?

It meant nothing.

In that moment, he knew everything Mandy had said was right, and he collapsed under the weight of the hypocrisy of his entire life. He had betrayed his ancestors to follow the white man's Jesus, and now his eyes were open to what he had done.

The Mother would show him the new way.

"L'vz'ratha! I call you!"

The last thing Innocent saw before everything went dark was Mandy's smiling face as she shrugged her robe off.

Innocent awoke sometime later in a comfortable bed, wearing satin pajamas. The scent of lilac and jasmine was in the air, and there was a sense of lightness and comfort around him that he had not felt before. Looking around, the room he was in was beautifully apportioned, with vases filled with various floral arrangements. Several open windows overlooked a wooded area. The sky was clear and the sun shone brightly.

Everything *felt* good, but yet he was still filled with trepidation. What had he done? Had he really forsaken God for some unspeakable pagan spirit? Had any of the events of the previous night actually happened, or were they all some fever dream, brought on by an unknown quality of the crystal they had discovered? In truth, Innocent knew nothing more than he had known the day before, much less any real answers about what was going on. The truth of the mysterious "L'vz'ratha" continued to elude him.

A knock at the door of his bedroom startled Innocent back into awareness. He was reticent to allow anyone to enter in as unprepared a state as he was, but he knew there would be no answers otherwise. "Come in," he nervously said.

Matthews walked through the door, holding a tray of covered dishes. "Good morning, Doctor. I'm glad to see you're awake. You gave us quite the scare."

"What do you mean?" Innocent asked.

"Why, you've been unconscious for eight days!" Matthews exclaimed as he sat the tray down upon a small table next to Innocent's bed. "Admittedly, the initiatory rite can be hard on the unprepared, but eight days seemed a bit extreme. Still, you're up and around. Mr. Dargaard will be pleased to hear about this."

"What do you mean, 'initiatory rite'?"

"Doctor, I know you're new to all this, but surely you can't have forgotten what happened in the sanctuary."

Innocent's stomach sank at those words; everything he'd feared had come to pass, and in a moment of weakness, he had denied the Lord in favor of some unknown creature. Shame burned through his body as the truth hit him, though he did his best to keep his true feelings to himself. He needed to know more, if only to stop what he was beginning to think was a dangerous cult from carrying out terrible plans.

"No, I have not forgotten. I just wasn't completely sure it was real." Innocent wasn't lying.

Matthews smirked at the response. "That's common, Doctor. The rite can be very…hard to swallow at first, but I assure you, it was quite real."

"What of the priestess I saw? Where is she?"

"Priestess? What do you mean?" Matthews was genuinely puzzled.

"The girl, the one with the dreadlocks and the tattoos. Mandy was her name."

"I'm sorry, Doctor, but there is no priestess at that sanctuary. Mr. Dargaard is the only one that tends it."

Innocent's blood ran cold. Who, then, was Mandy?

Innocent sat outside of the large chateau that he had been told was a residence for members of the Church, looking over the immaculately-tended flower gardens, staring at the small golden cross that he had worn almost constantly since he had become a Christian. Did this symbol have any meaning to him anymore, now that he knew he was so weak-willed that the wiles of a woman could sway him away from the Lord of All? He desperately wanted to fall to his knees and ask God's forgiveness, but could there be forgiveness for such betrayal? His heart ached with remorse at his failing, but he feared the judgment of the Almighty. Still, he would be judged regardless of whether or not he repented, so it was his choice as to which path he would follow. Two lay before him; either repent and return to God's grace, or follow the depravity of L'vz'ratha.

His heart wanted to return to the path of God, the road that made sense, where the world was a sensible six thousand years old, and forgiveness was possible through Christ's sacrifice, and so he uttered a quiet prayer as he sat there with the sun on his face, and the fragrance of a thousand blooms swirled around him. It all told him that God was there, in all things, and that this Mother was a false god, a fool's idol, and nothing more than that. He smiled, rejoicing in the hope that his soul wasn't irretrievably lost to L'vz'ratha's depredations.

"A lovely day, isn't it?" A familiar voice spoke from behind him, the voice of Gerald Tyler. "We'll be departing soon for Iraq. Don't worry about travel papers; those are already taken care of by our benefactors."

"Is it safe for us to travel there?" Innocent asked, concerned.

"The site we'll be going to is secure," Tyler replied, "as is the landing strip we'll be flying in to. We have boots on the ground in a lot of places, and once we knew where we needed to go, we moved resources to secure what we needed. We displaced some archaeologists, but they will be…compensated."

"Mr. Tyler, may I ask you a…personal question?" Innocent asked.

"I suppose, but let's be brief."

"Are you…part of the Church?"

Tyler chuckled, one of the very few times Innocent had seen him show any sort of levity. "One of the things, Doctor Nsabimana, you will learn quickly is that members of the Church will usually not discuss it outside of Church activities. You would do well to do the same."

Innocent nodded silently, realizing that Tyler had told him volumes without saying anything.

"Come, we have a plane to catch. Ur awaits, Doctor."

Chapter Seven

The plane voyage to Iraq was uneventful, with the weather being essentially clear and free of anything but the occasional turbulence. This proved to be a bane for Innocent, however, as it gave him to reflect on the events of the past few days. He was still quite unsure of what exactly had gone on, as well as being unsure of the loyalties of the people he had met over the last few days: Tyler, Matthews, Dargaard, Kombo, and now the others that were accompanying Tyler and himself on this expedition to the site of Ur, the ancient capital of Sumeria.

First, there was Elaine Hawkins, a sullen young woman who seemed to radiate despair and anger at all times, even when she claimed to be in a good mood; Austin Harridan, a man who seemed a little too close to the edge, one who almost could be thought to snap at any moment; and finally Anne Spencer, a woman who was Hawkins' polar opposite, who was possessed of an icy demeanor, and showed as little emotion as possible. All were accomplished archaeologists that Innocent had read papers by in the past, and all were archaeologists that had decided that Innocent Nsabimana was a crackpot at one time or another, regardless of his work.

Matthews piloted the aircraft that carried them from Geneva to Baghdad, and throughout the entire flight, he spoke to no one but the occasional tower that contacted them. Something seemed to be on his mind, something besides the flight, and even though he piloted more than competently, Innocent was concerned that it might mean trouble later on for him. Few things had meant good news since Tyler had hired him for the expedition, and he'd become hypervigilant about the little details.

They landed on a remote airstrip not far from Nasiriyah that the Church apparently had set up when the discovery of the location of Lucifer's fall was made. A gentleman attending the airstrip advised Tyler upon disembarking that a major sandstorm was approaching within a couple hours, and that the expedition would not be able to go to the dig site until the next day. Irritated by the delay, Tyler took a jeep from the airstrip's vehicle store and brought the team into town, checking them into the Sumerion Hotel.

The American members of the team seemed to get some odd looks as they checked in, but money talks; the clerk at the front desk was more than cooperative, finding enough rooms for each to have private quarters for the night. Innocent was glad of this, greatly desiring to have time to himself, time to think, time to pray for his salvation.

Innocent found the room comfortable enough, if not up to the standards he'd experienced in Geneva. Outside, the wind howled as the *haboob* whipped through Nasiriyah. It was odd for him to be so close to the place where the first known civilization had taken root, the place where the first true city and the first known written language had been found. There was so much there, hidden in the sands, so much history, even just in Ur alone, never mind locations like Babylon, Uruk, and the other sites scattered throughout Mesopotamia. He wondered silently if he himself would end up lost in the sands, or if God would find him in that desert expanse.

Would God find him before L'vz'ratha did? He just did not know.

Innocent fell to his knees before his bed and prayed in earnest, but he wasn't sure God could even hear him anymore. As the sands howled around him, he felt only one thing; isolation.

ᛋᚌᛝᚭᛁᚱᚦᛁᚭᛀᚷᚻ†ᛂᚱᛁᚨᚻᚱᛁᚠᚴᚱ†ᚻ

Morning came, and the storm finally subsided, and the city began to dig itself out of the sandy mess that had been deposited upon it. Fortunately for the expedition, they had parked in a mostly-covered structure, and were able to drive out once they have checked out of the hotel. There was a palpable tension in the air, however. Everyone felt it; it was as if the air itself had become elastic, and was being stretched to its limit. Everyone knew what they were doing was of the most serious import, and there was no mirthful camaraderie to be had on this journey.

Finally, they reached the site of the great ziggurat of Ur, which stood above them in all its glory. One of the oldest structures in human history, the ziggurat loomed above them, even as a mere shade of its former splendor. It was impressive, both as an archaeological site, and as a triumph of human ingenuity. Innocent had never seen the ziggurat before, and he now saw why he should have a long time ago.

Tyler rummaged around in a satchel that he had carried with him, and finally pulled out an odd-looking device, one that seemed to be crafted of a similar metal to that of the sanctuary doors, but newer-looking. He swept it in a wide arc in front of him, and it emitted a rasping sound, similar to that of a Geiger counter, which became faster and louder when pointed at the ziggurat.

"Of course..." Tyler mumbled.

Tyler waved Matthews over for a quiet conference, and eventually they waved Innocent over as well. Innocent joined them, not completely certain of what was going on.

"It looks like we have to go into the ziggurat, Doctor," Tyler whispered. "What we're looking for appears to be underneath it."

"Are we thinking of damaging it?" Innocent asked, horrified.

"We may have no choice, but only as much as is absolutely necessary," Matthews interjected. "I assure you, this is potentially even more of a discovery than Ur."

"It…it is understood," Innocent nervously replied. "Please try to do as little harm as you can."

Matthews followed the sound emanating from the device as it led them onto the stairs leading up to the top of the ziggurat. The sound grew steadily in frequency and volume as the approached the apex of the structure, until they reached the top of the second tier, where it became a steady tone. Matthews nodded to Harridan, who pulled a small device out of his pack, a device that looked suspiciously like an explosive. Harridan tucked the device into a small crack in the burnt brick facing of the ziggurat, likely where small arms fire had damaged it, and advised everyone to stand back and turn away.

A few seconds later, a sharp bang was heard, and a flash was seen as bricks were thrown free from the structure, torn from the Neo-Babylonian bitumen that they had been set in. Innocent winced in horror at the thought of such an ancient structure being defaced in such a way, but once the smoke and debris cleared, he was shocked to see what looked like some sort of metallic tunnel, with an entrance awaiting them, and the rungs of a ladder attached to the wall of the tunnel itself. Such a thing was impossible, and yet there it was, right in front of them.

"There it is, my friends," Matthews slowly said, as if in awe. "The way into the very tomb of the Anu'naki themselves."

"I…I don't believe it…" Innocent whispered.

"Believe it," Harridan interjected. "The apostates, the mutineers, those expelled from *Mr'ra*…they sleep beneath us."

Matthews idly chuckled. "You have to excuse Harridan. He's a true believer in the Mother. He *claims* he's felt her touch."

Harridan smiled beatifically, and then suddenly turned to Innocent. "I'm not the only one. You…you've *seen* her, haven't you? You *have* felt her touch too, yes? The girl with dark violet eyes?"

An icy chill ran up Innocent's spine. Was this crazy man talking about Mandy?

"He's a little loopy, but he gets the job done every time," Matthews continued.

"Assuming you can stand the sermons," Hawkins spat.

"It is true, he never stops preaching her gospel," Spencer added.

"Would you all just *shut the fuck up*?" Matthews barked, shutting everyone down quickly. There might not be anyone at the site right now, but I do want to get this shit done before anyone decides to go poking around to see what all the noise is. *Do we have an understanding?*"

No one spoke. No one dared.

"Good," Matthews continued. "Now. Harridan and Spencer, you're in first. Hawkins, you're in with me. Nsabimana, you bring up the rear. Let's move!"

The ladder leading down into pitch black was wide enough to allow two to climb at once, so the team went in twos. The metal, again, was similar to that of the sanctuary doors, having lost the green luster that the temple still possessed. Though the rungs of the ladder were smooth, the dry desert air prevented any moisture from condensing on any of the metallic parts, so the descent was not as dangerous as Innocent had feared, though he was alone, descending into the dark after the rest of the team.

Innocent also found the supreme irony in his descent into the underworld after what he'd done. Perhaps he belonged in Hell. The nagging doubt ate at him with every rung passed, far more agonizing than any physical discomfort he experienced.

For an unknown amount of time, they descended into darkness, but after what seemed like eons, they finally came to a source of faint light, and ultimately, a floor. The tunnel ended in what looked to be a large, hemispherical chamber, dimly lit by an unknown source of light. Around the base of the hemisphere were bizarre hieroglyphs of an unknown nature that ran all the way around the room. Otherwise, the chamber was empty beyond open doorways in front of and to the left of them.

"Alright," Matthews whispered. "Harridan, Spencer, Doctor Nsabimana, you go through the left door. Hawkins and I will take the one straight ahead. Meet back here in fifteen minutes."

Spencer visibly rolled her eyes at the assignment, but otherwise there was no further discussion on the matter, and the two teams went in their separate directions. Innocent clutched the flashlight Matthews had given him as if it were his lifeline to the surface, and to freedom. In a way, it was, for it was the only relief from the oppressive shadows that seemed to dance around him, just out of sight, out of the corner of his eye, maddeningly teasing him, taunting him to join them in their dance. Harridan took point as they quietly crept into the adjoining chamber.

In the next chamber, they found a similar hemispherical room, though smaller than the first. Small pillars of dazzling blue and red crystal were placed around the edge of the room at regular intervals, sparkling in the bright beam of the flashlight. More of the strange hieroglyphs could be seen around the base of the hemisphere, just behind the crystal pillars. In the center of the chamber, a statue of a bizarre creature, one that seemed to be half human and half bird, stood, its pedestal also emblazoned with the same hieroglyphs.

"My God…" Innocent whispered, barely audible.

"L'cy'ferr," Harridan said, his voice seeming to echo from all sides. "The prince of the Anu'naki."

Innocent turned to Harridan, an expression of puzzlement on his face. "You…can read…that?"

Harridan laughed. "That? Hell no! *She* told me who that is! She would tell you too if you would listen, but you cling to your false god so tightly. He can't save you. Only *she* can. Surely you know that now."

Innocent backed away from Harridan slowly, his hands shaking with fear. "No. I can do all things through Christ who strengthens me."

Harridan's jovial smile twisted into a cruel grin of malice. "Says the one who quakes in terror." He closed the gap between Innocent and himself with a small leap. "Let me tell you the story of the fall…the *real* story. Many eons ago, so long ago that none recall just how long ago it was, there was a world between Mars and Jupiter, a world its inhabitants called Kehl'la. It came to pass that a rogue planet found its way into the solar system, a planet they named Tiama't, the Destroyer, for lo and behold, Tiama't was on a collision course straight for Kehl'la. To save their species, the Kehl converted themselves into transdimensional beings, beings of pure energy that could be stored indefinitely, to be released when their storage vessel, called *Mr'ra*, found itself on a suitable world. In time, *Mr'ra* found its way to Earth, but the Kehl found it unsuitable, populated by savages…us…and too great a risk. A large portion of Kehl, led by L'cy'ferr, however, chose to leave the safety of *Mr'ra*, and descend to

Earth, to rule over the savages as gods. Thus, they became known as the Anu'naki; the apostates. The Anu'naki were foolish rulers and squandered the resources of the land, so the humans turned to the one, the only one, that could stop such powerful beings."

Innocent resisted saying the name, but his lips moved anyway. "L'vz'ratha."

"Yes! The one true god in the universe! Those men who called upon her formed her Church on that day, whose responsibility it was to seal away the Anu'naki for all time. Sadly, we lost track of where they were actually kept over the centuries…until now. Thanks to you, they are found…and now we have the means to *end* them for all time."

"You're going to kill them?" Innocent asked.

"Yes," Harridan said, pulling a .45 pistol from a shoulder holster and lovingly stroking it. "They die just as easily from a bullet to the brain."

"This…this is insanity!" Innocent protested.

"This is our duty," Harridan replied.

"Guys, this is sapphire," Spencer chimed in, examining one of the crystal pillars.

Harridan holstered his gun and went over to Spencer to get a closer look. He smiled with the mad smile of avarice at the sight of the sparkling gemstone pillar in the light. "It *is* written that the Anu'naki found great wealth deep within the earth, hidden from the eyes of man. Not anymore, motherfuckers."

Spencer checked her watch, remembering the time frame to which they were to adhere. "We have about three minutes before we're supposed to meet up with the other team. We better head back. We can make plans later about excavation once we clear out the den."

Innocent stood with his eyes wide, aghast. "You're all murderers!"

Harridan grabbed his gun and placed the barrel right to Innocent's right eye, and crowded in close, his face close enough for Innocent to smell his sweat. Harridan snarled with rage. "No. NO! You have it *backwards*! We are here to *stop* the *real* murderers, because we're the ones *chosen* to stop them. *So don't. Ever. Call. Me. A. MURDERER!*"

Trembling in abject terror, Innocent nodded in agreement, and Harridan put away his weapon. "Good boy. Now, let's head back like the lady said, alright?"

Once more Innocent nodded, too terrified to speak. He followed behind the other two, keeping as much space between himself and Harridan as he could without being completely separated from the group. He didn't know what he was doing here anymore; though the discovery of a clearly extraterrestrial installation underneath Ur was truly a monumental find, he had the suspicion that it would never be made public, and he wasn't there for archaeology anyway. He was there to kill…Satan? Lucifer? Such a thing was just nonsense to someone whose faith was certain, but with all he had seen, all he had learned over the past few days, Innocent's faith was shaken to its very foundations, and he was beginning to think that perhaps Lucifer was, in fact, an alien, and there was no god but L'vz'ratha.

As ludicrous as such thinking was, what else explained everything? If he was a man of science, as he liked to think of himself, as well as a man of faith, both dovetailed completely here in this stygian realm of demonic bird-men and shapeshifting nightmare creatures. A famous movie quote said that archaeology was the search for fact, and the facts said that the devil was from outer space.

The facts said that the name for god was L'vz'ratha.

The Mother of Madness.

It was at that moment that Innocent felt something *wrong* touch his mind, something malevolent yet craved him at the same time. It desperately wanted him to touch back, to reach out through the aether and make a complete link with it, and for a millisecond and yet an eternity, Innocent almost did, choosing to resist at the last possible moment. He knew what was happening; the Mother was calling to him, bringing him into her fold as she had Harridan. She wanted to break him, shatter his psyche, and mold him into another one of her monsters, a killer for the sake of killing. He resisted, but it took everything within him to do it. He did not know how long he could do so.

Moments later, the three had returned to the main chamber, but Matthews and Hawkins were nowhere to be seen. Even after waiting five more minutes, they hadn't shown, and the larger team became somewhat concerned. Spencer suggested that they go search for the other team, and Harridan and Innocent both agreed, so they went through the other doorway, hoping to find their missing comrades.

Inside the adjoining chamber, a terrifying sight greeted the three explorers; thirteen massive sarcophagi, each easily one-and-a-half times the height of a human, seemingly cut out of what looked like obsidian. The corners and sides were razor-straight, and looked sharp enough to slice through soft tissue should someone be foolish enough to touch them. The sarcophagi were arranged in a rough circle, with one even more massive one in the center. A few lines of the alien hieroglyphs were the only decoration on each, varying slightly on each; Innocent assumed that these were the names of their occupants.

Hawkins and Matthews stood near the central sarcophagus, staring in awe at the massive obsidian construct. Matthews turned to the approaching group, a broad smile on his face. "Can you believe it? This is it! Here they are, all of them!"

Harridan grinned and jogged quickly over to meet Matthews, gun in hand. "Let's crack it open and get this party started!"

All five put on thick gloves that had been packed in with their gear, and began shoving on one side of one of the outer sarcophagi. After several minutes of hard heaving and pushing, the massive stone slab atop the sarcophagus finally started to move. Though it took nearly half an hour to do it, they finally managed to push the slab off of the sarcophagus, which fell to the ground with a massive crash, one that echoed throughout the massive complex of chambers.

Now gathering around the sarcophagus, the team looked inside to see the horrific sight of a creature that was neither man nor bird, but a bastard hybrid of both. Its facial features were aquiline in the extreme, and there were what looked like talons were fingernails should be. Massive wings with brilliant, viridescent plumage enveloped its body as if it were a flower awaiting a chance to open. To Innocent it looked just like the statue he had seen in the other chamber; terrifyingly so.

"Which one is this?" Hawkins spat.

"If I compare Church stories to popular myth, probably N'r'gahl," Matthews responded, still barely above a whisper. "One of L'cy'ferr's lieutenants."

"Was," Harridan snarled as he pulled the hammer back on his weapon and aimed right between the eyes of the creature. He coldly pulled the trigger and the sound bellowed throughout the entire complex, echoing many times. The creature never moved, nor opened its eyes; only a gout of blue liquid pouring from the entry wound suggested that it was ever alive in the first place. "One down," he said, spitting a gobbet of saliva onto the creature's corpse.

"Come on, let's get the big one," Matthews said, sounding far less reverent.

Another half-hour of struggle resulted in removing the top slab, but inside there was something unusual; a smaller, coffin-like box made of the same greenish metal that Innocent was starting to find was becoming ubiquitous. It, however, was hinged, so they attempted to open it. Alas, to no avail; the coffin had been welded, or otherwise sealed, completely shut.

A plan was concocted to lift the coffin from inside the sarcophagus, and then use the small battery-powered bone saw that Harridan carried to cut through whatever was keeping it shut, and then access it. It was difficult removing the coffin; it was immensely heavy and awkward to handle. Once they had it out, though, Harridan went to work, cutting through the hinges in minutes.

"Time to see the face of the devil," Harridan chuckled with cruel glee as he opened the coffin.

Inside they saw…nothing.

Chapter Eight

"He's supposed to be here, Matthews!" Harridan screamed, desperation rising in his voice. "Where's he at? Where the *fuck* is he at?"

Everyone who had a sidearm drew, scanning the area for any sort of movement, but found none. The only sound was the echo of their own voices. Matthews raised his hand, indicating that everyone was to remain silent and keep eyes and ears open, but it was unnecessary; no one could utter a word, and no one could possibly open their eyes any wider than fear had already opened them.

Matthews signaled for the team to make their way back to the ladder, and the team slowly, silently, started to move. Matthews led, with Spencer directly behind, then Hawkins, Innocent, and Harridan bringing up the rear. Each covered as much of the room as they could as they moved, making sure that nothing could sneak up and take them by surprise.

"Wait." Hawkins suddenly said, stopping the team dead in their tracks. "You hear that?"

Innocent strained to listen and could just barely make out the sound of something heavy and wet dragging itself along, but much faster than it should be. He felt his blood run cold and electric chills run up and down his spine as he recognized the sound.

Matthews suddenly vanished behind one of the sarcophagi with a choked scream, and that was enough to cause the others to scatter and run for the exit. Hawkins screamed one word before gurgling into silence: "*VEN!*"

Hawkins' scream was enough to shake Innocent out of his fugue state, and he ran. He ran as fast as he possibly could, Spencer and Harridan right behind him. Without warning, though, a shadowy form leapt from a darkened spot in the chamber and tackled Spencer, who then vanished seemingly into thin air. By the time they reached the ladder to the surface, all that remained were Harridan and Innocent. The dragging sound was close; the gnashing of teeth and the unholy snarling of the Ven were far too close.

Innocent turned to the ladder and made to climb, but Harridan grabbed his arm first. "Not…quite yet." He brought the butt of his gun down on Innocent's temple and Innocent was unconscious before he hit the floor.

Some time later, Innocent woke in a different chamber, secured to a cold metal table with some sort of metal binds. The metal that he could see was silvery, and seemed to shimmer with an odd, almost fluid, quality. A strange apparatus was attached to the ceiling above him, with several armatures, each ending in some sort of instrument or tool. He could see nothing else in the room besides a large door comprised of the same silvery metal.

With a swishing sound, the door opened like an iris, the petals folding neatly into the wall. Through the new aperture walked a cleaned-up Harridan, dressed in a clean, dark suit. This was not the Harridan Innocent had seen deep underneath Ur; he was completely sane and calm.

"Doctor, I regret the means under which we had to…meet…but alas, I was not expecting to have to hurt poor N'r'gahl," Harridan said. "But we have long overdue for a conversation."

"What about Matthews, Hawkins, and Spencer?" Innocent asked, becoming quite upset as he struggled futilely against his bonds.

"They had to die. Enemy combatants in a very, very long war."

"I don't understand…"

"No, you don't." Harridan said, nodding. "But you could. Let me explain. But first…" He waved his hand towards Innocent and the binds dissolved into nothingness. Harridan smiled, an almost genuine grin. "I always love doing that. Now, where to begin…well, first of all, I'm not really Austin Harridan. My name is actually quite long and hard to pronounce, but I tend to shorten it to L'cy'ferr. I, as you may know, am a Kehl. However, the story you were told originally is bullshit. It's the story I fed to the Church to keep them off our asses when we're regenerating ourselves. We're not immortal, not at all, but we live for centuries and can live for a very long time with regeneration technology given to us by the Mother. You weren't supposed to find this place. Ever."

"I got that impression from the Ven watchdogs," Innocent said, a little sarcasm coloring his voice.

"Yeah, they do their job well."

"So, why kill N'r'gahl?"

"Let's just say he was naughty."

"Why don't you look like N'r'gahl?" Innocent asked, now genuinely curious.

"Physiological re-engineering. I physically rebuilt myself as a human. I'm actually what you would call female, but your barbaric, patriarchal little planet necessitated that I make myself male. It's actually very odd getting used to having a penis. What do you do with this thing when you're not using it?" He laughed heartily at his own joke, even though Innocent was slightly aghast.

"So, the Anu'naki aren't actually apostates?"

"Absolutely not! We are the greatest of the servants of the Mother! Why do you think I am seen as a bringer of light? The light lures them to the Mother's judgment, and she touches whom she chooses. And she has chosen to touch you, Doctor, but you resist. Why?"

"Why? I felt her touch, and it felt *wrong*, like the most horrible thing imaginable trying to burrow into my mind."

"Pardon my vulgarity, Doctor, but you fucked a Ven," L'cy'ferr said, a sly smile on her face. "I can't think of much more horrible than that."

"I won't surrender. Not to you, and not to her."

L'cy'ferr shrugged. "It doesn't matter much to me, but I'd hate to be the one that denies the Mother what she wants. She will have it, no matter what. Free will is not assumed here, friend."

With that, the feeling of *wrongness* returned, only it hit with the force of a hurricane. The world as Innocent knew it shattered, and everything was just *wrong*. Nothing was the way it should be; L'cy'ferr was gone, the room was gone, and Innocent was alone, lost in a black void that felt infinite. He felt like a microbe under the lens of a very great microscope, and his every move, his every thought, was monitored.

"Don't you get it yet, Innocent?" the familiar voice of Mandy asked from behind him. "You've been running from something you can't run from. How can you hide from something that is *everywhere*? How can you elude something that knows all? How can you defeat the will of a *god*?"

"There…there…is…" Innocent trembled with fear, quaking far too much to complete a sentence. "There…is…only…"

Mandy put her arms around Innocent's torso from behind him, embracing him gently, and laying her head upon his shoulder. "You're right, Innocent. There *is* only one god. It's just *not* the one you thought it was."

"I…I…don't understand…" Innocent stammered.

"You've been fed lies your entire life, from your birth until the day you first encountered Gerald Tyler. Your mother, your ancestors, your American teachers, your professors; all liars. And they were all lied to as well. Back through the generations to a point lost in history where a man could not accept that the supreme god of all things could be anything but another man. I believe Abraham is what you would call him; I call him the first liar."

Clutching his head as pain began to well up within, Innocent fought the urge to scream. Mandy stroked his short, close-cut hair gently as she moved close to his ear. "She told him to kill his son not because she wanted a sacrifice, but because she simply wanted him to kill the little brat."

Innocent tore away from Mandy, trying to move, trying anything to escape from her, half mad with terror. The pressure within his head was unbearable as the Mother bludgeoned him within his very consciousness, trying to force her way in. He stumbled over his own feet and fell, his eyes never leaving his tormentor, whose kindly smile seemed like that of a shark.

"You can't run anymore, Innocent," Mandy said, her pleasant smile and enticing eyes far more predatory than before. "She has need of you. She *will* have you. Give in."

"Never. *NEVER.*"

"It will hurt more if you fight."

"Then it will hurt more."

"Like you hurt everyone you've ever known? Like you sacrificed everything you've ever had for foolhardy red herrings?"

Innocent was confused by this; what did she mean by bringing up such things?

"You were engaged once, weren't you? Except you ran away to America to pursue Christ…and you didn't even say good bye to her, did you? And what about your family, who still don't know what happened to you? You threw away all of this, for a *lie*. For smoke and mirrors, Innocent. You can't even live up to your *name*, can you?"

Stunned, Innocent fell to his knees, silent and in terrible pain, no longer needing to scream. Instead, he began to sob, to cry.

"She knows all these things…but it's not too late. These can all be made better, Innocent. The slate can be wiped clean." Mandy walked over to the sobbing, broken man, laying a hand atop his head. "Give in. Let her touch you, and every mistake, every harm you've done, will be undone. You will be her messenger, her scholar, her voice to the world."

The broken, shattered man could say nothing; he could only nod.

ᛁᚱ Ο Ν Ǝ ᚲ Ν Ο ᚤ ᚠ �

The world reformed around Innocent, but this time his heart was light. He was clean, he was pure, he was made new in the sight of God. L'cy'ferr nodded respectfully to him as he rose from the floor, sensing the change.

"She has a message for you, dark prince," Innocent said, a different look in his eye than before, a look that seemed to stretch on to infinite madness.

"Do tell?"

Innocent smiled broadly, the kind of smile that only the truly disturbed ever smile. "Wormwood."

OTHER BOOKS BY

BRITNEY EVERLONG

TREE OF DEATH

JERICHO ROAD

BIRD OF PARADISE

BLOOD ROSES

ALLISON'S GAME

HUNGER

ALL-AMERICAN DEAD GIRL

www.ingramcontent.com/pod-product-compliance
Lightning Source LLC
Chambersburg PA
CBHW061320120726
48001CB00002B/609